"Maybe t
me."

Walker ached to pull her close. "There is nothing wrong with you, Rebecca. You are perfect." He wanted to lean in closer to her, but it wasn't his place. He was just a friend. One with an unwelcome connection to her ex.

"How would you know?"

"Because I knew Vince, and I know you."

She shrugged, not believing him.

He lifted her chin and looked into her beautiful eyes. "Rebecca, the reason I told you about my family is that your past relationship with Vince doesn't have to determine your future. You can make a fresh start. And you have family, right here in Eden, ready to help."

"But I'm not real family."

He laughed. "I dare you to tell Aunt Bell you're not real family. Just as Aunt Bell took us in, we've taken you in. You can start fresh here."

"A fresh start, huh?" A small smile tugged at the edge of Rebecca's lips.

At the look of hope with a dash of uncertainty in her eyes, he gave in to all his instincts and pulled her close. The sweet smell of lemons enveloped him. He felt the pressure from the day ease.

"A fresh start."

Alena Auguste lives in Texas and can't imagine living anywhere else. She's married to her very own knight for thirty plus years, and she and her husband have four amazing grown children and two of the handsomest grandsons ever! When she's not creating trouble for her characters or working at the family business, you can find her cozying up with a steaming cup of tea and a good book. She would love to hear from you at alenaauguste.com.

Books by Alena Auguste

Love Inspired

A Family on His Doorstep

Visit the Author Profile page at LoveInspired.com.

A FAMILY
ON HIS DOORSTEP

ALENA AUGUSTE

LOVE INSPIRED
INSPIRATIONAL ROMANCE

LOVE INSPIRED®
INSPIRATIONAL ROMANCE

ISBN-13: 978-1-335-62106-1

A Family on His Doorstep

Love Inspired
22 Adelaide St. West, 41st Floor
Toronto, Ontario M5H 4E3, Canada
www.LoveInspired.com

Printed in Lithuania

MIX
Paper | Supporting
responsible forestry
FSC® C021394

Now unto him that is able to do exceeding
abundantly above all that we ask or think,
according to the power that worketh in us.
—*Ephesians* 3:20

To My Family,

To my kiddos—Joshua, Caleb, Eden, Faith—
and my beloved daughter-in-law, Mackenzie:
love you all so much! Thank you for your
encouraging words that kept me going.

Clyde, thank you for your support. I love you, Babe.

A big shout-out to my writing friends:
Tari Faris, Rachel Hauck, Lisa Jordan, Beth K. Vogt
and Susan May Warren. The GLAM Girls—
Gabrielle Meyers, Lindsay Harrel and
Melissa Tagg—as well as Mary Bell and
Jeanne Takenaka. Thank you, ladies, for the years
of prayer, laughter, encouragement, brainstorming
sessions and, most importantly, the gift of friendship.

To the FFC Ladies—you know who you are—
thank you for being my cheerleaders!

To my editor, Melissa Endlich, and the team
at Love Inspired, thank you for guiding
this newbie author patiently through the process.

To my agent, Rachel Kent,
thank you for your guidance and support.

Most importantly, Lord Jesus,
thank You for allowing me to live this amazing life.

Chapter One

❧

If she were any other person, she would have trashed everything in the box.

The burn of rejection still stung as Rebecca Young stared at the box of Vince's things in the passenger seat. He'd literally walked out the door when she told him she was six weeks pregnant. He'd mumbled that he was sorry but wasn't ready to be tied down and left. Instead of a happily-ever-after, she got a slammed door and pictures of him with another woman on his social media account.

She parked her car next to the picture-perfect southern Texas house, Vince's home. Maybe nobody would be there, and she could leave the box on the front porch. Yes, that was what she'd do. She'd drop it off and disappear, closing this chapter in her life.

She got out of the car and retrieved Vince's things. She hadn't been able to toss them in the trash. Just thinking about it hurt Rebecca's heart, and she forced the sob back. Vince had walked away without looking back, but she couldn't. Two weeks after he left, he was dead. Car accident, they said. She would never know why he chose to leave her.

Gritting her teeth to keep the emotions at bay, she walked up the steps under the full glare of the summer sun. If the mile-long driveway lined with crepe myrtles or the immaculate house with rocking chairs on the wraparound porch didn't tell her she was out of her element, the gleaming white F350 truck she parked next to would have. Her ancient beat-up car seemed like a tin can next to that monster truck. She set the box by the front door. Before she could take a step back, the door swung open.

Vince's mother, an older version of Jackie Kennedy with silver hair, stood in front of her dressed in a white cardigan, soft pink silk shirt and tan slacks. Rebecca and Vince had dated for two years, but she'd only seen Vince's mother one time, and that was at a distance. He'd never introduced them. She looked so different from her Aunt Grace, who was a tiny Trinidadian woman.

"Can I help you?" The woman opened the screen door and stepped out, a kind smile on her face.

Rebecca fidgeted with her hands. "Um, I wanted to drop off some of Vince's things."

The woman's eyes immediately watered. "Oh, how kind of you." She reached out a hand. "I'm Vince's mother—Bell Greystone."

She couldn't help but shake her hand. "Rebecca Young."

"Won't you come inside? If you were a friend of Vince's, I'd love to visit for a little bit. In fact, why don't you stay for Sunday lunch?"

"Um—"

"Aunt Bell, who's here?" a voice called from the house. What was Walker doing here? His voice brought back bittersweet memories of fun-filled Sundays watching football games at her apartment in Houston.

"It's a friend of Vince's, Rebecca Young. She's brought some of his things for me."

"Rebecca?" Walker Greystone stood in the doorway, then stepped onto the porch. Tall and proud, all six feet of him.

His brown hair and chiseled jaw looked the same as the last time she'd seen him. Only then his smile had been friendly, his face full of laughter. But not now. Now, his eyes seemed full of questions. He let the screen door slam shut and stood next to Bell. He wore his signature polo shirt, faded jeans and work-worn cowboy boots.

Bell appeared oblivious to the sudden tension between them. If the way Walker glared at her was any indication, he obviously knew Rebecca and Vince had broken up before his death. And wasn't that just great. Someone else knew about her humiliation.

"Honey, will you get that box and show Rebecca in? She's joining us for Sunday lunch. I'm going to get some refreshments while we wait for everything to be ready. That way we'll have some time to visit." Bell disappeared into the house.

"What are you doing here? I thought you and Vince broke up." Walker said, hands on his hips, head tilted to the side in question.

Yep, he knew. This was the last thing she wanted. But she couldn't be rude to Vince's mother. That was one thing she'd learned from her Trinidadian father, to respect her elders. A trickle of sweat ran down her back as the breeze shifted. Rebecca appreciated the breeze but immediately regretted how it exposed her baby bump.

"You're pregnant?"

She looked at Walker then down at her belly. Her entire reality exposed.

This was why she shouldn't have come. Walker knew they broke up but not about the baby. Did Vince's child matter so little? She straightened her shirt and stood tall even though everything in her wanted to curl up in a ball. "Yes, I'm pregnant."

She walked past him and entered the house. She refused to feel sorry for herself or get lost in the swamp of the emotions trying to drown her. Her focus needed to be on getting a job, securing a place to live and raising her child. Alone. She was done with men, especially any man with the last name Greystone.

Walker grabbed the box and followed Rebecca into the house, the quiet hum of the air-conditioning in sharp contrast to the questions echoing around in his head. Her black curly hair brushed the shoulders of her denim shirt as she stopped and turned to him. He paused before realizing she didn't know where to go. How could she? She'd never been here before. And why was that? In all the time they'd been a couple, why hadn't Vince brought her home to meet the family?

"This way." He took the lead as they passed the formal entry way and walked into the family room where Bell had decorated with well-used coffee-colored leather couches. He set the box next to the coffee table that held Aunt Bell's favorite hydrangeas. He indicated for her to have a seat just as his phone buzzed. Walker wanted to ignore the text and question Rebecca, but when he pulled out the phone, it was his brother, Grant. It had to be about the library bid, a job they desperately needed. "Can you excuse me for a second?"

She nodded.

He stepped into the hallway. He didn't want to miss the conversation between Aunt Bell and Rebecca. But this bid was important to the future of the family contracting business, Greystone Home Services. He'd been entrusted with leading the business. The library bid was due first thing tomorrow. Walker wanted it submitted via email tonight so it would be the first thing they saw Monday morning.

He dialed Grant. "Hey, what's up?"

"Are you sure you want to put in a bid for the library job?" Grant asked. "Commercial air-conditioning is a lot harder than residential."

"This is our shot to work with JC Construction," Walker responded. "If we get this job with them, it will open doors for more commercial work." Walker paced as he answered. He didn't want to worry Grant. It was his job as the oldest brother to take care of his siblings. They had to become the HVAC contractor of choice for JC Construction in order to support their business through the winters. Though locally owned, JC Construction was the top commercial contractor for the tri-county area. But he didn't want to worry his brothers. "Grant, we need commercial jobs for the slow season. At this rate we won't be able to support our families if we don't."

Grant laughed and asked, "What families? You're still single buddy. And with your level of grumpy, you will be for a while."

Walker dragged his hand through his hair as he paced. Taking a quick peek at Rebecca, he saw that she sat ramrod straight, tension oozing off her. "Ha-ha, a comedian. You better submit it quick and get over here. You don't want Aunt Bell mad because you're late for lunch." Walker whispered.

He ended the call and slid the phone into his back pocket. If they could get this job as a subcontractor on the library remodel, it could springboard them into more commercial air-conditioning jobs. The library job alone would get them through winter. One more like that this year and they could buy the truck they desperately needed. He glanced back at the living room. Now they may have a baby to support. He'd promised Uncle Hank, Bell's late husband, he would look after Vince. He'd failed when Vince moved to Houston, determined to get away from small-town life. At the time

Walker thought the best course of action was to give Vince space. One year had turned into two, and now Vince was gone forever. But he wouldn't fail Aunt Bell or Vince's baby. He heard Aunt Bell moving around in the kitchen. He only had a few minutes before she returned to the living room to get answers from Rebecca.

"Sorry, I had to answer that. Work stuff."

"On a Sunday?"

"When you own a family business, work never shuts off. Because Greystone Home Services covers remodeling and all the trades, we are always on call."

She nodded. The only thing breaking the silence was the clattering dishes as Aunt Bell prepared the serving tray.

Walker cleared his throat as he leaned against the Austin stone fireplace. Rebecca sat on the couch, her hands clenched together. Her baggy blue shirt hid the baby bump well. Normally, everything about her was open, friendly, and warm, but not today. He pinched the bridge of his nose. Vince told him they'd had a nasty breakup. Rebecca didn't seem like the kind of person to lie, but he trusted his cousin. Maybe...

"Whose baby is it?"

If possible, her posture got straighter as a tinge of color rode high on her cheeks.

The heat of her side glare burned. "Vince's."

"That's not possible."

She turned toward him. "It is. I told him. He left me. The next thing I knew he was killed in a car accident."

Pushing away from the fireplace, Walker paced. "He just walked away?"

She gave him her profile again. She swallowed but nodded. "Yes."

"I don't understand." Walker raked his hands down his face. Family took care of family, always. They were taught that from early on. How could Vince simply walk away from his child?

"I didn't either. I thought we were going to make a family together. I was obviously wrong. A mistake I won't ever make again." She stood. Straightened her top. "Please tell his mother that I couldn't stay but I appreciate the offer." She'd almost made it to the doorway before he stopped her.

"You can't just leave," he whispered so Bell wouldn't hear. He was determined to keep all stress away from Bell. It was the reason he moved back in after Vince died.

"I can. I am. I don't want to hurt his mother. She's been through enough. Nor do I want her to think I want anything from her. It's bad enough Vince didn't want his own child."

"It's Vince's baby?" He swung around and saw Aunt Bell standing there, wringing a dish towel in her hands. Her pale face was a reflection of the shock she'd been dealt. The same shock he'd been denying since he saw Rebecca on the front porch.

He nodded to Rebecca to have a seat. He was relieved when she walked back and sat down. Her hands once again in her lap, clenched tightly but at least she hadn't bolted. He guided Bell to the couch.

"Walker, is this true?" Bell gripped his arm as she sat down, pulling him down beside her. He would rather pace than sit, but he had to consider his aunt.

Rebecca's face was deadpan, but her eyes were full of pain, something she wouldn't want him to know. But after hanging out together for two football seasons, you learned to pick up on things. He'd visited Vince in Houston, and they inevitably ended up at Rebecca's apartment to watch football. She'd cook and study while they talked during the game. He ran his hand down his face, the other still held in a tight grip by Bell.

"Walker?" Bell questioned.

Instead of outright rejecting Rebecca's words, he squeezed Bell's hand. "Rebecca and Vince were dating when he lived in Houston."

"So, it's true?" Bell's eyes brimmed with tears. His aunt lost her husband, Uncle Hank, unexpectedly two years ago, and she just lost her only son four months ago. Now this. He worried it was too much for her to bear.

"I think Rebecca is the best one to answer that." They both turned to Rebecca. Aunt Bell's face was filled with sorrow, and determination to know the truth.

"Yes, ma'am. Vince and I dated for two years. We broke up shortly before his death." Her gaze and voice were steady as she answered.

"The baby… is his?"

"Yes, ma'am. You don't have to worry. This little guy will be well taken care of." Rebecca patted her belly with a smile stretched across her face. The first real expression of joy he'd seen since she arrived.

"It's a boy?" Bell's tears covered her cheeks. "A boy. You're carrying my grandson."

He ran his hand through his hair. No way would Vince deny a child. Would he? He'd changed so much once he left their small town of Eden, Walker couldn't know for sure.

"Ma'am, I—"

"Call me Bell, honey. You're family now."

Rebecca stood. "I didn't mean to upset you. My only intention was to return Vince's things. I…um…have to go. Thank you for the offer of lunch."

Bell walked around the coffee table. She gripped Rebecca's hand. "Why do you have to go?"

"I have to get ready for an interview tomorrow." Rebecca shifted from foot to foot.

"An interview? Where? Back in Houston?"

Rebecca pushed her hair back behind her ear. "I'm interviewing for a part-time library position. Here."

"Here in Eden?"

"Yes, ma'am. My friend Carrie David lives here, and she told me about the opening. That's how Vince and I met actually."

"I see. Carrie, the Davids' daughter?"

"Yes, ma'am."

"I see. That job must be the one that my friend Rachel mentioned. I didn't realize they'd posted it already. Where are you staying?"

"I booked a room at the Inn. I wanted to drop off his things and then prepare for the interview tomorrow." Rebecca shifted her eyes to look at him. He could tell she was confused by all of Bell's questions.

"Oh, no, you shouldn't stay there. It's just not safe. You can sleep here. No family of mine is overnighting at that place. Why, just last week our friend, Deputy Brian Arnold had to lock someone up for disorderly conduct in the lobby."

Aunt Bell turned to him. "Walker, get her bag from her car, and I'll set her up in the mother-in-law suite."

"No, really, I—"

Bell patted Rebecca's hand. If the situation wasn't so serious, he would laugh. But he knew that there was no way Aunt Bell would allow Rebecca to leave her sight.

"We have so much space here at the ranch, honey. It's not a big deal. Besides, we must think of the safety of you and the baby."

After a long pause, Rebecca finally gave in. "Well… all right, thank you." Aunt Bell had raised five boys in her household. She was strong-willed and could get anyone to do anything she wanted before a person even realized she was doing it.

Bell patted the hand she was holding. "Perfect. Now, let me show you to your room while Walker gets your bag. Don't just stand there, Walker. Go on." He nodded and jumped up off the couch.

"This way, dear. It's perfect timing. Walker's brothers are coming over for Sunday family lunch in about an hour, so you can meet everyone." Walker didn't hear Rebecca's response as she and Aunt Bell disappeared around the corner that led to the bedrooms.

What was really going on here? He needed time to figure it all out. And having the woman who claimed to having his late cousin's child here, even overnight, would help him get answers. Plus, he was certain Aunt Bell would be devastated if Rebecca left with her only grandchild.

If this truly was Vince's baby, he would figure out a way to keep the baby close.

Chapter Two

Rebecca followed Bell down a hallway lined with family pictures on the walls.

Bell swung open the door to the mother-in-law suite. "It's more like a mini apartment, really. I had it added added after my husband, Hank, passed away. It was always my dream to live in the same house, help with the grandkids, but be independent. I thought that time would come soon, but—"

Rebecca's heart hurt as Bell brushed tears off her cheeks. To give Bell some privacy and let her gain control of her emotions, Rebecca stepped into the suite. It was open concept with a small living room decorated in grays and blues, with yellow accents. A compact kitchen was set up on the left side of the room, separated by a seating area with a table two chairs. Farther in, she could see a bedroom and closet.

"It's beautiful, Bell. Thank you for allowing me to spend the night." Rebecca was torn. She was glad to save the money, but she didn't want the Greystone family to think she was here to take advantage.

Bell pulled her into a hug. "No, dear, thank you. If you hadn't been kind enough to drop off Vince's things, I would never have known about you or my grandson. You have my thanks." Bell gave her one more tight squeeze and fanned her face. "Okay, enough of that. No more tears today." She sniffled and headed to the door. "Lunch should be ready in about an hour. So, feel free to have a little lie-down. I'll have Walker set your bag outside the door so he won't disturb you." Bell was gone before she could reply. Rebecca swallowed, her heart heavy for what could have been.

The peaceful lake view through the sliding glass doors drew her attention in direct contrast to the riot of thoughts running through her mind. She shook her head, glad that no one could see her.

Just then there was a knock at the door. When she opened it, she found her bag but no Walker. She was glad for the reprieve. What must he think of her? What had Vince told him about their breakup for Walker to look at her with distrust?

Rebecca wheeled her suitcase roller bag into the bedroom and laid it on the edge of the queen-size bed. Over the four-poster bed hung a picture of a rolling pasture with cattle. On the opposite wall was a flat-screen TV. She pulled out her makeup case and took it to the bathroom counter. Against the bathroom wall stood a full-length mirror. She stopped to look at herself. What must Bell think? At six months pregnant, the baggy shirt hid her baby bump; it was loose and comfortable for the hour-and-a-half drive from Houston. If this was the reaction of Vince's family today, she could only imagine the reaction from her own family. She winced. Aunt Grace, in particular.

She patted her belly. The little guy had been quiet today, not moving around much. "Don't you worry, buddy. We are going to be okay. Momma's going to get a job and find us a place to live." Her eyes felt gritty from the strain of the day. She glanced at her watch. A short nap would help her face the rest of the family. She toed off her shoes and collapsed onto the comfortable mattress. She should enjoy these accommodations while she could. She had no doubt that between her low bank account and hopefully a part-time job, she'd be living on ramen noodles for a while. That was if she aced the interview tomorrow.

Rebecca's eyes popped open suddenly. She rubbed the sleep from her eyes as she checked her watch. Oh no. It'd been an hour! She slid off the bed and put on her shoes. After checking her face in the bathroom mirror to ensure she had no sleep lines, she hurried out. She didn't know exactly where she was going, so she followed the voices she heard. Bell found her just as she entered the living room.

"Rebecca, there you are. Were you able to have a nap?"

"Yes, ma'am. Sometimes, I'm more tired than I realize. I hope I haven't kept you-all waiting."

Bell waved her concern away. "Sunday lunch is informal. It's just family. Besides, I set out a loaf of fresh bread on the kitchen counter. I'm sure the boys already helped themselves, even though they're not supposed to." Bell motioned for her to follow. "Come this way. We'll no doubt catch them already snacking," Bell whispered as they rounded the corner to the kitchen. She wriggled her eyebrows and put a finger to her lips. "Shhh." Before she could respond, Bell stepped into the open-concept kitchen and asked, "Walker, Robert, Grant, Parks—are you-all eating already?"

The guys stood around the bread platter, the evidence still in their mouths. Bell wagged her finger at them. "You boys know good and well, you're supposed to wait until we're all seated to eat."

Rebecca locked eyes with Walker and attempted to keep her laughter to herself. He swallowed the bread in his mouth as his aunt stopped directly in front of him. It was good to see him off balance for a change.

Bell shook her finger. "Especially you, Walker. You're the

oldest. You're supposed to set the example." From where she stood, Walker tried to look repentant but failed. Miserably.

Rebecca couldn't help but grin.

Each "boy" in the kitchen topped six feet. They had the same build as Walker, with varying shades of brown hair, except for the little blue-eyed boy with dark curls, held by one of the giants. "Gammy, I told Daddy you say no. But Daddy say it okay."

Bell kissed the boy's head as he slipped from his father's arms to his great-aunt. "It's okay, Bentley. Gammy isn't mad at you."

Bell shifted Bentley to her left hip and proceeded to move the platter out of their reach. Bell winked at her as she set the half empty platter on the table. Bell strapped Bentley into his high chair and motioned to the group.

"Rebecca, let me introduce you to the rest of the Greystones. This little guy is Bentley." Bell attached Bentley's plate to the high chair with suction cups.

Rebecca waved, and he waved his little plastic fork at her. Her heart clenched. Is this what her son would look like?

"He belongs to that big lug over there—" Bell pointed to the man in a dark blue plaid shirt "—Robert."

Robert reached over and shook her hand. "You can call me the Big Lug as opposed to the Little Lug you already met—Walker."

Walker elbowed Robert and received a glare from Bell. "Boys, please."

Rebecca could feel their deep affection for one another. It was nice to be part of a family. It was something she's always wished for.

"The man standing next to him is Grant." Dressed in a green short-sleeve button-down shirt, Grant stepped up and shook her hand. Grinning, he said, "Don't worry, no lug here. I'm the smart one in the group."

The next brother chuckled. Twin dimples greeted her as he shook her hand. "I'm Parks, the handsomest of the group." She hid her grin behind her hand as the rest of the brothers groaned.

"Okay, everyone, let's eat." Bell sat at the head of the table. The men seemed to sit in assigned seats, and she waited to see which chair remained empty. Bell motioned for Rebecca to sit on her left. Bentley sat to Bell's right and then Robert. Grant slid into the seat next to him, with Walker at the other end of the table. Parks pulled out her chair before he took the seat next to her. Bell reached out her hand on both sides and bowed her head.

Vince's family were people of faith. Her shoulders sagged in relief.

Rebecca saw each of the brothers do the same. She clasped Bell's hand and bowed her head.

"Dear Lord, thank you for this food we are about to eat, and thank you for bringing Rebecca to us. In Jesus' name, amen."

After a quiet round of amens, Bell passed a huge platter of fried chicken, followed by colossal bowls of mashed potatoes, green beans, and gravy. The smells made Rebecca's mouth water, reminding her she hadn't eaten since that morning.

It was silent as everyone dug into their food. Bentley stuck his fingers in the potatoes and licked them. Bell handed him his fork without missing a beat and gave him a mock glare, which only made him laugh as he pounded the fork in and out of his mashed potatoes.

Rebecca swallowed. This would soon be her, responsible for another life. Feeding her child.

"How far along are you?" Parks asked before he bit into a piece of fried chicken.

She almost choked.

Walker frowned at his brother. "Please excuse Parks's bad manners."

"Bad manners? We know she's expecting, and we all want to know when—so why not ask?" When no one responded, Parks shrugged and dug back into his mashed potatoes.

She glanced around the table. All the faces turned toward her, and she could feel the heat of a blush rising on her cheeks. She hated being the center of attention. Taking a sip of her sweet tea to gain some time, she finally answered. "I'm in my second trimester, around six months along." She set her glass on the edge of the place mat. "It's a boy."

Bell squeezed her hand, a shimmer of tears in her eyes. "I'm glad you decided to come to Eden. Boys, Rebecca has a job interview tomorrow."

Rebecca nodded, the tightness in her stomach increasing. The interview. So much was riding on her making a good impression and securing the job.

"Where?" Grant asked as he swiped the last slice of bread from the platter.

"The library here in town. My friend Carrie David told me about an open part-time librarian position." Her bank account needed an influx of cash soon. She'd put most of her things in storage in Houston until she got settled. Until then she'd kept her most essential spices and seasonings and kitchen gadgets with her, hoping to save money by cooking her own meals with the second hand hot plate she purchased.

"Why Eden?" Robert asked as he added another spoonful of mashed potatoes to Bentley's plate.

Walker leaned his head back and waited for her answer.

"Honestly, I graduated with a Masters of Library Science last month, and I've been on several interviews. But, well, nobody wants to hire someone pregnant. Carrie told me about this position in town and said she could put in a good word for me." The uncertainty of her future frightened her, but she didn't want the Greystones to know. "So here I am."

"What? They can't not hire you because you're expecting!" Bell gasped, horrified.

"No one's said that exactly, but it's easy to guess. I graduated top of my class and am available to start work immediately, but it's the same every time. I did great on the phone interview and the Zoom interview. But the in-person interview, well, I get the same response after they've met me in person—they've already filled the position."

"That's terrible," Bell said as she wiped Bentley's face free of mashed potato.

"I didn't think the qualifications were stringent for a library position to just shelve books," Parks commented around a mouthful of fried chicken.

"Most places require a master's degree to qualify. That's why I stayed in school to finish my master's degree. And being a librarian requires a bit more than just shelving books." She laid her fork on her plate and sat back.

"Seriously?" Parks raised his eyebrows as he reached for his iced tea. Based on his demeanor, he seemed the easygoing one of the bunch.

"Seriously." She took a bite of the bread.

"Books?" Little Bentley asked as he pounded his spoon on his high chair tray.

Bell nodded, and Bentley clapped his hands. "Hungy, Hungy Katepilla!"

Bell slid Bentley's bite-sized chicken pieces onto his plate. "We love *The Very Hungry Caterpillar*. It's our favorite naptime story. Bentley, Rebecca is going to work in the library."

Bell moved her hands to show the opening and closing of a book. "The place with the books. We take him every week for Toddler Tuesday." Bell wiped Bentley's face again.

"Aunt Bell volunteers there. Voluntarily." Parks shuddered. "A room full of twenty screaming two- and three-year-olds is not my idea of a good time." He looked over at Rebecca. "And you want to work there?"

Robert laughed. "We barely handle Bentley when he throws a tantrum, much less twenty kids at a time. You are one brave woman."

"I love books, and I love kids. It seems like a dream job to me."

Bentley clapped his hands. "Hungy, Hungy Katepilla."

She hoped the library job would work out, but hope had yet to find her. One look at the state of her life revealed just how precarious her future was. She needed that job, and fast.

Otherwise, she wasn't quite sure of her next step.

Walker scooped another heaping serving of mashed potatoes onto his plate. Parks asked another stupid question. He grimaced and shoveled more food in his mouth to keep from groaning out loud. Hadn't he told them to be friendly, make polite small talk and make her feel comfortable? But did his brothers listen? Of course not.

If she didn't run back to Houston today after lunch, that would be a victory. Walker pushed the green beans to the side of his plate. He still had to find out why Vince had abandoned his child. Even if he didn't want to marry Rebecca, why abandon her? And why not tell the family about the baby? It seemed so out of character for his cousin.

"Aunt Bell, do you know anything about the library position since you volunteer there so much?" Robert asked as he helped himself to the last fried chicken leg.

"I know they have a part-time position open, but I haven't really heard much about it. I'll make it a point to find out more tomorrow." Aunt Bell turned to Rebecca. "Why don't you and I drive into town tomorrow, and I can show you around?"

Before Rebecca could respond, Walker jumped into the conversation. "That would be great, Aunt Bell. I can check on the Nelson job and head to the library when it opens. You know it's best to catch Beth first thing in the morning." He looked over to Rebecca to explain. "Beth Porter is the librarian."

"Did you submit the library bid, Grant?" asked Robert.

Grant pushed the mashed potatoes around on his plate. "Yeah. I'm still not sure about taking on commercial jobs, though. The liability is more than we've ever had. It'll require more stringent permits and higher insurance."

"It's necessary," Walker responded. "We need to become JC Construction's HVAC contractor of choice. A few jobs with them will see us through the slow season. We talked about this already, bro. Besides, it's Sunday. Let's leave business for tomorrow." Not to mention they had to discuss how to finance the service truck they desperately needed.

Rebecca cocked her head. "What library bid?"

"The town received a grant to remodel the library, and they are completing it in phases. The biggest commercial construction company in town is JC Construction. He's picking the air-conditioning contractor this week. Our company put in a bid to do the HVAC portion of the remodel. They're supposed to announce the winning recipient this week."

"Walker is determined to beat the other company and expand Greystone Home Services to commercial. Then we'll be Greystone Services." Parks stretched to give Walker a fist bump. With Parks being the youngest, Walker knew his brother didn't understand the risks.

"Walker and Don Graves, the other contractor, have been at odds for years," Parks went on. "It started in elementary school and went through high school."

Aunt Bell frowned. "It's best to let that go, Walker. Unforgiveness will keep you chained to the past."

Walker turned his glass of sweet tea in circles on the table. It wasn't old news. It was ancient news. Small towns excelled at long memories. Eden, Texas, was no exception. Don made sure to keep the old gossip alive. Every time he thought they had forgotten the Greystone history, someone mentioned Walker's alcoholic father or grandfather again. He glanced back at Rebecca. It wouldn't be long before someone filled her in. She'd probably want to run after discovering more about their family. Especially the way Vince let her down. Walker would have to be the Greystone to step up and honor commitments.

"Rebecca, dear, don't be shy. There's plenty," offered Bell.

Rebecca patted her tummy. "I couldn't eat another bite. Thank you for lunch, Mrs. Greystone. It was fabulous." Walker hoped a full stomach and the banter around the table put her at ease. Maybe he could find out the reason Vince left. "I can see why Vince spoke highly of all of you," Rebecca said as she set down her glass of tea.

"Yet he never said a word about you. If it wasn't for you dropping off his things today, we'd never know about you or the baby," Robert said. His words sounded loud in the silent kitchen.

Rebecca froze. She never could play poker. Her face showed all her emotions. At first, her expression was confusion, but Walker could see it soon morphed into hurt.

He glared at his brother and turned to her, but she avoided

his eyes. While they were all shocked at Rebecca's appearance today, Robert was being overly harsh. Walker understood why Robert was jaded given the difficulties he had with his late wife. He tried to think of something to say but couldn't. Rebecca folded her napkin, put it on her plate, and stood.

"Thank you for lunch. I appreciate it. It's been a long day, and I need to prepare for tomorrow." She pushed her chair to the table and fled.

"Great going, Robert," Walker hissed.

"It's the truth, Walker. He didn't tell us about her," Robert muttered.

"So, why tell her that? Just because your ex was trouble doesn't mean Rebecca is. Where is your common decency? Huh?" He jumped up from the table, his boots echoing off the hardwood floors.

"Rebecca, wait." He caught up with her as she started to shut the door. "I'm sorry for what Robert said."

She whipped around to face him, fire in her eyes. Good. Walker preferred anger to tears.

"Why? He only spoke the truth."

Walker ran his hands through his hair. "Look, all of us are still reeling from Vince's death. It's barely been four months. And I knew you and Vince were dating, but nobody else did. You showing up here today, well…" He gestured toward the baby bump.

"Be honest, why would he mention me? I obviously didn't matter to him." Rebecca crossed her arms.

He understood the defensive move for what it was. He sighed. Vince had always wanted something other than small-town living especially for the last couple of years. It's why he'd left Greystone Home Services and the ranch, and kept contact with the family to a minimum. Never did he

think that Vince wouldn't return. So why was it so unbelievable that Vince would abandon his own child?

He didn't want to believe that of his cousin. Walker
couldn't take his eyes off Rebecca, and her pronounced baby
bump. He could see she wasn't lying. She was devastated by
Vince's action, yet she'd dropped off his things. She didn't
have to. She didn't come here looking for a handout.

He needed to help her. It was the right thing to do. Besides, it would devastate Aunt Bell to lose her only grandchild, and that's what would happen if Rebecca left town and
went back to Houston. He blew out a breath.

"I'm sorry I've doubted you. And I'm sorry Robert was
rude." He stuck out a hand. "Truce?"

Rebecca stared at his hand.

"We will figure this out, one way or another. Let's focus
on you getting the library job, and we can go from there."

She reached out and shook his hand. Barely. Could he
blame her?

"I know it's been a long day. You're right, you should rest.
Tomorrow, I'll drop by the library and talk with Beth Porter,
the librarian. I can put in a good word for you. That's who
your interview is scheduled with, right?"

Rebecca crossed her arms in front of herself but nodded. "Yes."

"Great. One of the best things about this town. Everyone
knows everybody. She was born and raised here." It was one
of the downsides of small-town living too. But he wasn't
about to tell her that.

"I'm going to let you rest up and I will see you tomorrow." He had to make sure she got that job. He was a man of
his word, and he'd promised Uncle Hank he'd take care of
the family. And he would do it in whatever form that took.

He just had to convince Beth to give Rebecca the job.

Chapter Three

Walker pulled open the library doors and left the oppressive Texas humidity behind in favor of the cool town library. He'd spent a restless night worrying; his mind wouldn't rest until Rebecca had a reason to stay in Eden. That meant a job.

Beth had to hire Rebecca. Vince had destroyed Rebecca's trust, and he had to win that trust back. For her and for the baby and Aunt Bell. And maybe even for himself.

He stopped in the wide entryway and slid his shades into the top of his blue polo. He wiped the sweat beading on his forehead. Yes, they were definitely ready for a new air-conditioning system. He spotted Mrs. Robin, one of the librarians at the front counter and headed that way. The faint whir of the photocopying machine in the background was the only sound that could be heard over the murmurs of the patrons.

"Good morning," Mrs. Robin said, her salt-and-pepper hair looking the same as when he was a youngster. "My, my, Walker Greystone. I haven't seen you in a library since you and your cousin pulled that prank when you were…what, ten years old?" Mrs. Robin looked at him over the reading glasses perched on the end of her nose.

"I promise you, I'm not here to pull a prank, Mrs. Robin. You're safe." He stopped in front of the well-used maple counter.

"Well then, are you here to sign up for the adult summer program?" Mrs. Robin asked, raising one eyebrow.

He caught himself before laughing out loud. He studied technical manuals, listened to marketing podcasts and read business books to help support the family business. Reading for pleasure was something he'd given up a long time ago.

"No, ma'am. I need to speak to Beth if she's around." He glanced toward the back of the library where a group of elementary-aged kids giggled over a book, their backpacks strewn in a semicircle on the green carpeted floor beside them.

"Let me check. By the way, any word on who got the AC bid yet? The days are getting hotter, and with the remodel, it's hard to keep our patrons cool in the afternoon."

"Not yet. They're supposed to make an announcement this week." He rested his elbow against the counter, its edges smooth from thirty years of kids and parents alike leaning against it.

"It can't happen soon enough." She reached for the phone. "Hold on one sec while I buzz her for you."

Not one to hover, he strolled over to the reserved section in the middle of the foyer. Three large metal shelves full of books reserved for patrons were stacked in the library's front entry for easy access. What it must be like to have time to read for pleasure. He reached for a hardcover book, *Traveling the World for the Adventurer*.

The love of travel was something he and Vince had shared. But he'd promised Uncle Hank before he passed that he'd take care of the family and their business, which meant staying close to home. He slid the book back onto the shelf, its title hidden once again.

Mrs. Robin put the phone down. "Walker, she's on the second floor, around aisle K."

He nodded his thanks, jogged up the green-carpeted stairs to the second floor.

He found Beth, wearing her trademark burgundy cardigan standing amid the tall aisles, a mobile computer cart in front of her and a cart full of books a foot away.

"Hey Beth."

She turned and pushed up her glasses. "Hey Walker, what are you doing here? I didn't think they were announcing the winning bidder yet."

He leaned against a shelf and folded his arms across his chest. "They aren't. I'm here about something else."

She raised her eyebrows past the rim of her glasses. "Must be important. I haven't seen you in the library since middle school."

He winked. "Technical manuals for HVAC systems seem to be my only reading material these days."

She wrinkled her nose. "Seriously? That sounds awful."

He shrugged. "It's all I have time for."

"Now that is truly sad."

He cleared his throat, anything to get the topic off himself. "I heard there was a part-time job for a librarian."

"Word travels fast. Are you applying?"

"Have you lost your mind? Inside for ten hours a day, five days a week? You know better."

She laughed. "That I do. It's fun to tease you, though." Beth blew out a breath. "It's only 10:00 a.m. and it's already been a day. I'm telling you, between the building renovations, shifting library sections to accommodate the construction, and the summer program—we are scrambling every day to keep up. To top it off, Lauren, one of the other librarians, decided she's not returning to work after she has her babies. But did she tell me herself? Nope. She told Mary Sue, and Mary Sue told me. Plus, I'm already short-staffed." She let out a huff. "Then the mayor called this morning. Do you know he wants to move our reopening to coincide with the Fair on the Square event in September?"

He scratched his head. "No, I thought the remodeling project wasn't supposed to finish until November."

"Yeah, well, he moved it up." She grabbed a book, checked the spine and put it in its place.

"Oh." He handed her the next book.

She took it and slid it in place. "Thank you. He told me at 7:45 this morning."

He winced. "Was that before or after your third cup of coffee?"

She drummed her fingers on the hardcover book stack. "Before I had my second cup."

Walker took a step back. "So, have you had your third and fourth cup yet?"

She waved him off. "Relax. I'm on my fourth."

"Um, considering he's the mayor, I hope you were at least civil with him."

"Oh, I was civil all right. Then he had the nerve to tell me his daughter was looking for a job, and would I please consider her." Beth shoved the cart farther down the aisle.

Walker scrubbed his hand down his face.

No. No. No.

He needed Rebecca to get this job, and if she had to compete against the mayor's daughter, the chances were slim. Very slim indeed.

"Does she have experience? None. Does he know a master's degree is a requirement for a librarian? No. How could he be so dismissive?" Beth threw up her hands. "Not to mention the pressure. I don't like politics in general, but small-town politics?" Beth grabbed a stack from the cart's bottom shelf and slammed them on top. "The worst."

This was a significant complication. Then again, when had anything in his life been simple? He'd all but promised Rebecca this job, with his personal recommendation no less.

Beth blew out a breath and adjusted her glasses. "I'm sorry, you didn't come here to listen to me rant. What's going on?"

"I, uh, wanted to talk to you about an applicant for the part-time job."

She tilted her head. "Wait, you know someone? That's a good fit? Here in Eden, Texas?"

He ran his hands through his hair. "She's Vince's girlfriend. Well, ex-girlfriend."

"Vince's ex-girlfriend? He had a girlfriend?"

"Confidentially. We didn't know about Rebecca or the baby until yesterday." He squeezed the back of his neck.

Beth held up a hand. "Vince had an ex-girlfriend who's pregnant and you-all didn't know?"

He held up his hands. "Yeah, and she's living at the ranch house with Bell and myself in the mother-in-law suite."

"And you want me to hire her?" Beth pointed to herself.

"Yes, she's having a hard time finding a job because she's pregnant. She's qualified—with a master's degree in library science."

Beth folded her arms across her chest and stared at him. "Did you just hear me say how much I hate small-town politics? There's one thing I detest even more. Know what it is?"

He shifted his feet. "What?"

"Small-town drama." She drew a circle with her finger between them. "And this has the makings of serious small-town drama."

He held out his hands in supplication. "Just talk to her— she graduated at the top of her class from the University of Houston."

Beth raised her eyebrows. "Really?"

"And she interned at the library in downtown Houston." He reached over and pulled the last bundle of books from the bottom of her cart and set them on top. "Please, Beth. All I'm asking is for you to give her an honest shot at the job."

Beth pulled one of the books off the top. "That's not all you are asking me to do, and you know it. To make it worse, Bell will ask me the same thing."

He shoved his hands in his jean pockets. "Probably."

Beth turned to him, her hand still on the spine of the book, *Troubled Waters*. "Tell her to apply and I can schedule an interview."

He swallowed. "That's the thing, she's coming in for an interview this morning."

Beth stopped, "Wait, Rebecca Young is Vince's ex?"

He nodded.

Beth groaned. "This day just keeps getting better."

He knew Beth was torn, and he couldn't blame her. He'd put her in a difficult position. Do him a favor or make the mayor angry.

Beth sighed. "I will give her a fair shot—that's all."

He held up his hands. "I totally understand. I want her to be considered on her merit."

"I can't make promises. You know, that, right?"

He nodded and gave her a fist bump. "I do." Just then, his phone buzzed. Pulling it from his back pocket, he opened his messages. "Gotta run. Work calls."

Beth waved him off.

He jogged down the steps. He didn't want to think about telling Rebecca the job might go to someone else. Much less to someone way less qualified for the position. It would be one more rejection, and she'd had too many of those lately.

How was he going to fix this?

What he and Beth both knew, but weren't allowed to address, was if the other full-time librarian, Lauren, did not return from maternity leave, the person holding the part-time position, would be next up to fill the full-time librarian position. But until Lauren officially told Beth she wouldn't be returning Beth had to hold the position open.

He needed that person to be Rebecca. The child she carried was Vince's. It would devastate Aunt Bell if she couldn't be a grandmother to her only grandchild. She loved Bentley, but Bentley was her great-nephew. Rebecca's child would be Bell's only grandchild and his cousin.

To top it off, there was something about Rebecca that always intrigued him. She seemed stable and sensible, a stark contrast to Vince's wildness. He'd had plenty of time to observe them the last couple of years and he'd always felt that Vince had leveled up with a woman like Rebecca. How could he have walked away from someone like that? He'd never understand.

Rebecca had too much riding on this job. It was her hope for a better tomorrow. Rebecca sat in the hard mauve plastic chair in the front room of the library as she completed the application form. She crossed and uncrossed her legs. She breathed in the smell of books as she studied the people milling around. Kids sat with headphones on in the rectangular computer room while several older patrons were seated throughout the library reading or working on their laptops.

The quiet atmosphere was something she enjoyed and had forgotten about in the race to find a job. She signed her name to the end of the application and flipped to the front to review what she'd written.

Everything was complete.

Should she hand it to the lady at the counter or ask to

speak to the head librarian? Checking the time, she was early by thirty minutes. Maybe she should just wait.

The front door opened, and a gust of warm air blew in with a smiling Bell. Her silver-streaked hair bounced with each step.

"Bell?" Rebecca stood up, the clipboard with the application in her hand.

"Hello, dear." Bell walked toward her, dressed in stylish slacks and a red-and-white polo.

Rebecca's suite at the Greystones' home had an automatic coffee maker and a separate entrance. She'd made herself some coffee to start her day, then headed straight here. She'd been glad not to run into anyone. Knowing she'd have to say goodbye to everyone later today, she was only delaying the inevitable. Plus, she had to make arrangements to stay at the Inn. Maybe she could crash at Carrie's until she heard whether she got this job.

"Bell, I'm sorry I didn't see anyone when I left this morning. As soon as I'm done with the interview, I'm going to pick up my things to head out. I want to thank you for your hospitality." She clutched the clipboard in front of her, uncertain of her reception after the way lunch ended yesterday.

"Listen, honey, I don't want you to worry. You stay with us for as long as you need. Beth won't make a decision today, so you might was well stay with us. Besides, that inn is downright dangerous."

"That's very nice, but I don't want to be a bother."

Bell shook her head. "You won't be a bother at all. In fact, that room is like a mini apartment. You saw how easy it was to come and go without seeing anyone."

Rebecca nodded. After a sleepless night, she was thankful to slip out unnoticed.

"That's why I built it that way. The boys are already over-protective of me. Goodness, they act like I'm old. I can't imagine what they'll be like ten years from now. That's why I created that suite with its own kitchen and separate entrance. Independence."

"But, I don't want…" She let out a breath. It was better to just face it head-on. "I don't want there to be any issues. I'm sorry Vince didn't tell you about the baby, but I understand everyone's concern. I'm not here to freeload from you or anyone else."

Bell stepped closer and squeezed her hand. "You would be doing me a favor by staying. Honestly, another woman around will help keep those boys in line. Plus, you will need help when your baby arrives, won't you?" The twinkle in Bell's eyes was irresistible. "My grandson."

How could she say no? Her own mother was dead. Vince was gone. This baby needed at least one grandparent who would be there for him. But if she didn't get this job, what would she do to support them? She was already six months along. Who would hire her?

"If I get the job, I'll stay, deal?"

Bell clapped her hands. "Deal.

"Now, follow me. Don't be nervous. I taught Beth, the librarian, in Sunday school along with the boys. She married John Porter, her high school sweetheart, and now she has three kids of her own. She's such a sweet young lady."

Rebecca followed Bell through a door tucked between the restrooms and the activity area. Her body broke out in a cold sweat when they stopped at a small office with a turquoise-colored wall lined with books. Photo frames on the credenza displayed pictures of three teenagers in a dance production. The lady who stood before her, a brunette with glasses, had to be in her early forties. Her piercing eyes made Rebecca want to fidget. What was she thinking? Did she see the baby bump and automatically disqualify her for the position?

"Beth, I brought you someone who I think will be perfect for the part-time librarian job. I believe she's already on your interview schedule. This is Rebecca Young. Rebecca, this is Beth Porter."

Beth stretched out her hand, and Rebecca took it. "Nice to meet you, Beth."

"The pleasure is all mine. It's not every day I have two visits from the Greystones." Beth gestured to the black plastic chairs in front of the ancient metal desk. "Please have a seat."

"I will leave you ladies to your interview. I'm going to visit with Robin. I hear she is expecting her fourth grandbaby. Rebecca, I'll meet you at the front desk when you're finished." Bell winked and breezed out the door.

Rebecca wiped her hands down her black dress slacks.

"May I see your application, please?" Beth gestured to the clipboard on Rebecca's lap.

"Oh, of course. I attached my résumé with the application." She handed over the clipboard and forced herself not to fidget. Interviews were tense. She should be a pro by now, not a bundle of nerves.

Beth flipped through the papers and sat back in her chair. "Tell me about yourself."

Rebecca folded her hands in her lap and tried to smile. "I completed my master of library science this May. I graduated in the top ten percent of my class."

"I see that." Beth ran her finger down the résumé.

"I also took several classes in grant writing to help the library where I used to work apply for grants."

"Why here?" Beth set the papers next to her computer and leaned forward, folding her arms on the edge of the desk.

Rebecca straightened, forcing what she hoped was a calm

smile on her face. "I'm sure you've heard by now that Vince Greystone is the baby's father." She took a deep breath and forced herself to continue. "Carrie David told me about this job opportunity, and after graduating my time was up in Houston, so I thought why not?" She didn't have any other options. But, of course, she couldn't say that in a job interview.

Beth nodded. "Yes, Carrie called and recommended you. You are quite popular. Not only did Carrie recommend you, so did Walker. He's positive that you would be great for the job, as is Bell."

That was good right?. Personal recommendations might tip the scales in her favor to get the job. She'd been pressured to complete college all her life and told a job would be a sure thing once she obtained her degree. Ha!

"Tell me about your volunteer work and practicum. As a small library, we need someone who is diversified. Do you have experience with either?"

"Yes, ma'am. I volunteered at a local library in Houston, and then I completed my practicum at the Central Library in downtown Houston. I also assisted during the summer reading programs."

"What did you enjoy most?" Beth flipped the pages again, making notes in the margin of her resumé.

"The children's reading program. We found a multitude of sponsors and incorporated hands-on activities. We increased the participation numbers thirty-five percent over the previous year."

Beth jotted something down beside her résumé while she asked more questions. Then Beth placed the paperwork inside a manila folder and closed the folder. Smiling, she stood.

Rebecca stood, too. This was it. The polite brush-off.

Beth stretched out her hand. "Thank you for meeting with me, Rebecca."

With the neutral expression on Beth's face, Rebecca couldn't tell if she'd done well on the interview or not. "Thank you for allowing me to interview."

Beth laughed. "This is Eden, dear. You didn't just have one recommendation but three. Plus, well when a Greystone makes a recommendation we tend to listen. They're one of the nicest families around. Besides, Ms. Bell is the only person who calls me young anymore."

Beth rounded the desk and gestured for Rebecca to follow her. But Beth stopped abruptly as she looked through the glass door that opened to the main library. "The mayor is back." Beth opened the door and ushered her into the main area, but stayed in the hallway, hidden from view. "He's already been here once today, and I have too much to do to try and put on a politically correct face right now, so I'm going to disappear before he sees me. You haven't been introduced to small-town politics yet. But don't worry, you will."

Rebecca's eyes darted to the tall, well-dressed man in the lobby and the librarian, unsure of what to say to that. "Thank you again for your time."

"You're welcome. Listen, I know you're new and it must be a little overwhelming, but Eden is a great town. It's a great place to raise a family and to make lifelong friends. Besides that, you've got the Greystones in your corner. They're good people."

The pressure in Rebecca's chest eased. Maybe the Greystones were actually rooting for her. From her brief exposure to Eden so far, she did like the town. It was all the unknowns in her life that made her feel inept. Lost.

"I will let you know about the position as soon as I can." Beth hurried back to her office.

Rebecca adjusted her purse on her shoulder. She headed toward Bell, who stood conversing with the balding man in a three-piece suit. He seemed out of place compared to the other patrons who roamed around the library in casual clothing.

Bell motioned her over. "Dear, I'd like you to meet Mayor Roger Stephenson. Roger, this is Rebecca Young."

He held out his hand. "Good to meet you."

"Rebecca just moved here from Houston. She is staying with us at the ranch."

"I hope you grow to love our little community as much as we do," said the mayor.

Rebecca shook his hand. "Thank you, sir."

Bell slid an arm around Rebecca's shoulders. "She just interviewed with Beth for the part-time librarian position."

Mayor Stephenson's eyes narrowed as his lips thinned. "That's interesting. I talked to Beth this morning about that same position. My daughter Denise is looking for a job."

Rebecca's hopes plummeted. Her competition was the mayor's daughter? *Lord, can I please get a break here?*

"Denise is looking for a job as a librarian?" Bell frowned as she waved a hand across the room.

He nodded. "She's coming home and plans to start a master's program online. Evelyn and I are positive once she gets a local job, we can convince her to stay in Eden."

Bell tilted her head. "Roger, I thought she wanted to move to a big city and model?"

The mayor pushed his horn-rimmed glasses up from where they'd slid down his nose. "She may want to, but we don't want her going far, and Houston is too far."

"It's quite a jump from a modeling career to a librarian, though." Bell folded her arms over her chest as she eyed him.

He shrugged. "Evelyn normally gets what she wants."

This must be what Beth meant earlier. Small-town politics. Rebecca tightened her grip on her purse as bile rose in her throat. How could she compete with the mayor's daughter? What would she do now?

She wiped the sweat from her brow. She couldn't call Aunt Grace and tell her she was unemployed, unmarried and pregnant. You just didn't do that, not where she came from. As a first generation American, the pressure to do everything right was intense. That meant college degree, job, marriage and then the baby. She gave herself a mental shake. She was in a new town and just finished an interview with personal recommendations. She would hope for the best.

Chapter Four

Walker knocked on Rebecca's door. It'd been a long work day and as good as the hot temperatures were for the air-conditioning business, he was ready for his day to end. His truck had broken down two miles from the customer's house. It'd been both embarrassing and expensive. The cost to repair the truck was quickly becoming crippling. He'd called to confirm JC Construction had received their bid for the library job while he waited for the tow truck. Shoving the financial worry to the back of his mind, he prayed, *Please Lord, grant us favor for the library job.*

The gallon of Blue Bell ice cream in his hand felt good in contrast to the heat. This flavor was Rebecca's favorite. At least it was during last football season, if memory served. Although he read somewhere that women's taste buds changed when they were pregnant. Maybe he should have called first? She opened the door, dressed in a soft pink jumper and flip-flops, her curly hair half up and half down. He held the ice cream in front of him as if he were a butler. "In the hopes of apologizing for our awful behavior yesterday, I come bearing the famous Blue Bell Mocha Almond Fudge ice cream." He handed it over with a flourish.

She clapped, her smile wide and her laughter happy and

free. He liked the sound of it. A man could get used to that laugh.

"Oh, my goodness, Walker! This is perfect. Come in." He followed her into the living room as the air-conditioning cooled the sweat from his forehead.

"How did you know what I was craving?" Warmth spread up his neck as she looked at him like he was some kind of hero.

"I remembered when I picked up some last minutes items for Aunt Bell from the grocery store today. I wanted to bring it by around lunchtime, but Ms. Thompson's AC went out and I had to go there first."

"I didn't realize you made calls yourself."

"One of our technicians called in sick, so I was helping out." Just then he sniffed the air, the smell of bread and roasted tomatoes wafted past him. "Wait a minute, did you make your famous tomato choka and roti?" He checked out the two burner stove and oven in the small open concept kitchen.

She grinned. "You weren't the only one in the grocery story today. I had a craving for some of Aunt Grace's staple Trinidadian meals. The ice cream will make the perfect dessert. Would you like to stay and have dinner?"

His stomach grumbled before he could answer. Rebecca grinned as she stepped into the U-shaped kitchen. "I'll take that as a yes."

"Can I help?"

"You can keep me company. Not much space for two people in this kitchen. Have a seat."

He slid onto one of the wood bar stools as Rebecca put the ice cream in the freezer.

"How did the interview at the library go today?"

"It went as well as can be expected. I actually stayed afterward. Bell showed me around the library and introduced me to some people."

"That was a good idea, get to know the layout of the place where you're going to work."

She whipped around. "Did you hear something?" she asked, her eyes wide open.

Great, Walker, way to get her hopes up. "No not yet, but I'm sure you'll hear some good news soon."

"From your mouth to God's ears," she said as she turned back to the stove.

He noticed a stack of books on the end table; one of them was the best places to travel in the United States. "You like to travel?"

"I hope to one day." She patted her belly. "It'll be a while before that happens though, with this little one coming soon."

He kept reading the spines of the stack of books on the table next to the couch. A daily devotional, a Bible and the book *What to Expect When You're Expecting.* The same one he downloaded on his phone last night. He knew next to nothing about pregnancy, children or parenting.

"How do you like the pregnancy book?"

At her questioning look, he pointed to the end table. "Oh, that one. I've never had a baby before, figured I ought to know something about it. It was one of the top borrowed books from the library in the pregnancy category."

"I've found it informative so far."

She pivoted toward him. "Wait, you're reading that book too?"

He froze. Should he have admitted that? "Well, yeah. I mean, I want to be able to help and I've never had a baby before either, so I downloaded it."

She gave him a wide, full smile. A smile that reached her eyes. "Walker, that is so sweet. Thank you."

Walker slid his hands into the pockets of his jeans, hoping for a casual response because he hadn't intended to reveal that. "I mean, we don't want you to be alone in this. We want to help you with the baby."

She reached out and squeezed his hand over the counter. "Well, I appreciate it. It means a lot that you would take the time to read that."

He nodded. He'd always been a little envious of Vince. Whenever he visited Houston, and they all hung out together, Rebecca always gave Vince her full attention. Why would Vince give up that level of devotion? He would never understand, and Vince wasn't here to explain himself.

Rebecca buttered the tawah, a flat frying pan he remembered her cooking on at her apartment back in Houston. "I made enough dough to make several rotis so there will be plenty to share." She flipped the roti and leaned the pan off to the side, pushing the roti toward the open flame in a circular motion. "Hey, I met Ms. Jennie in the library foyer as I was leaving. Aunt Bell introduced us. She came by to drop off books with the cutest little girls."

"Breck and Gracie?"

"Yes! While they were picking out books for their summer reading, she told me some stories about you."

Walker dropped his head in his hands. "No, please tell me she didn't."

Rebecca nodded. "Oh, but she did."

Her eyes twinkled as she slid a roti on a plate, covering it with a dish towel. "She told me about you and your brothers' antics from kindergarten to high school."

"Uh-oh." Walker could feel the heat travel up his neck and groaned.

"Yep, she told me you were crowned prom king and your date, prom queen."

"Yeah." Walker rubbed his hand along his jaw. "Clara was my first serious relationship."

"How long did you date?"

"Through high school and college. Seems like forever ago."

Rebecca shook her head. The light caught her dark curls as she moved around the small kitchen. Right now, she didn't seem sad or tired. This version of Rebecca was well rested. He was glad some of the bags under her eyes had disappeared.

"Why did you guys break up?"

He swiped at imaginary crumbs on the counter. How honest did he want to be with her? And would she open up about her relationship with Vince? "Just didn't work out."

"Boy, do I understand that."

The pain was evident in her voice, but it didn't sound like she'd put a wall up like yesterday.

Rebecca slid another roti under the dish cloth and turned to put the last one on the pan. Good thing she was busy, because he didn't want her to read his face. He still remembered the day Clara called it quits. While she wasn't the hardest end to a relationship, Veronica was. He'd thought his broken heart would never heal after Veronica. He'd put his all into the relationship, thinking she was the one. Her laughter had cut him to the core when he asked what she thought their future looked like. He'd gripped the promise ring that burned in his front pocket while she laughed at the prospect of a future for them in Eden.

"Walker, can you grab the place mats? They're in the drawer to the right."

"Sure thing." He grabbed the mats out of the side drawer and put them on the two seat dining table. Rebecca served the tomato choka and roti. The aroma of the fresh-cooked roti was amazing. Fresh bread was always a win with him. He hadn't eaten since a cold breakfast burrito this morning, and his stomach growled again. He grinned as it echoed between them.

"I'm obviously ready to eat. Let me grab the drinks." He got out two bottles of water from the fridge and set them on the table. He pulled the chair out for her to sit.

"Would you mind saying grace?" she asked.

"Sure thing." He took a breath. This moment seemed like something he could do every day. Coming home to dinner with a beautiful woman. He held her hand, soft and feminine, and bowed his head. He had to remind himself, this wasn't for him. Based on the actions of his father and grandfather, he knew he wasn't made for a relationship. Especially with Rebecca.

"Lord, thank you for this meal and for the hands that prepared it. Bless it and bless the little guy growing inside of Rebecca. Thank you for bringing them to us here in Eden. Amen."

"Thank you, Walker." Her eyes glistened.

"Thank you? You haven't even had the ice cream yet."

"No, I mean thank you for your support. It really means a lot."

The truth was, he was helping because it was Vince's baby. He wanted to help her get a job nearby or Aunt Bell would be devastated.

He tore a piece of roti, soaked it up in the tomato choka and took a bite. "So good! I've missed eating this."

She smiled. "I'm glad you like it. Vince didn't like much of the Trinidadian food I cooked." She tore a piece of roti and tore it again.

Seeing the dejection in the droop of her shoulders, he knew it was time to change the subject. "Everyone knows

I'm a risk-taker when it comes to food. It helps that my buddy in college was from Jamaica. He took me to this hole-in-the-wall restaurant deep in Houston that had the best jerk chicken I've ever tasted."

"Ever?"

He grinned. "Okay, so it was the only jerk chicken I've tasted. But it was really good."

She grinned. "I see what you're doing."

He scratched his head. "Eating?"

"Uh-huh. You're trying to change the subject. Tell me more about your ex-girlfriend Clara."

"Honestly, Rebecca, there's nothing to tell."

"Come on, Walker. Spill it."

Shifting in his seat, he picked up another roti and soaked it in the sauce. "Honestly, it wasn't Clara but Veronica who was the bad breakup. She had plans that didn't include me or Eden, Texas. And this place has always been my future. No way would I ever turn my back on Uncle Hank, Aunt Bell and my brothers."

She tilted her head to the side. "No regrets not pursuing her?"

He shook his head. It was one thing he was certain of. He would always choose family over himself. Clara and Veronica had both wanted a big city life like Vince. But his life and responsibilities were in Eden. "None."

Rebecca savored the last of her ice cream as Walker washed the dishes. He was a man who worked for a living, and you could tell by his broad shoulders, muscled chest and strong calloused hands. She couldn't help but compare the difference between Walker and Vince. Walker focused those sea-blue eyes on her while he listened, giving her his full attention. Vince would text while talking to her, barely acknowledging her, especially toward the end of their relationship. Maybe the signs were there that he'd lost interest; she just hadn't noticed. Walker shifted to place a dish on the drying rack.

"Walker, I think we should discuss the elephant in the room."

He dried the last dish, set it in the cabinet and shook his head. "Rebecca, I hate to tell you, but there is not enough room to house an elephant in this place."

She rolled her eyes. "Seriously, we need to talk about what happened on Sunday."

He leaned back against the counter and paused before he said, "Okay, let's talk."

She traced the place mat's checkered pattern. She knew he had plenty of questions. She had her own questions about why Vince walked away from her, but for the time being she had to deal with this. After a long pause, she finally said, "Nothing is going to change the fact that I'm pregnant with your cousin's baby. I have to be adult enough to accept that the relationship for whatever reason didn't work. You said Clara and Veronica wanted something different than you did. I thought Vince and I were on the same page." She shook her head, swallowing against the knot of emotion in her throat. Now wasn't the time to break down, especially in front of Walker. "I'm not sure I'll ever understand why Vince left me, but I'm committed to moving forward. Once I'm settled with a job and good place to live, I will move on. I don't plan on being in this position forever. I hate being a charity case. I need a job. It's the only reason why I considered coming to Eden."

Walker pulled a chair out and straddled it, his long legs taking up the space between them. "You are not a charity case. Besides, I've been around enough to know you will succeed. This difficulty in finding a job is just temporary."

"Be that as it may, I want to be clear. I don't expect anything from you or Bell or the rest of the family. I know there's competition for this librarian job as well. If it doesn't work out, I will contact my aunt."

"Did you tell her about the baby yet?"

"No, but I will if I don't get this job." She really didn't want to. She sucked in a shaky breath, the thought of making that phone call. The shame that call would bring nearly overwhelmed her.

"I know you interviewed well. I fully expect you to get hired. Besides we don't want you to move. We hope you stay here and raise the baby on the Greystone Ranch."

He wanted her to stick around? Wait, no he said "we." Did that mean the family? Did that mean they didn't want her around, just the baby. Why did that make her feel less than? "Walker, you do know the mayor wants his daughter to get that job, right?"

"Yeah. But Beth is a strong person, and she is passionate about the library. She won't let politics get in the way of hiring the best person."

She let out a sigh, troubled. "If you say so."

"I do. You'll see. Have a little faith."

Rebecca squeezed her hands together. Problem was, she didn't know if she even had a mustard-seed-size bit of faith right now. How long would it be before she was told she didn't get the job? How long before she had to move on or call Aunt Grace for help?

Chapter Five

Walker parked in front of the Greystone offices as the first streaks of dawn filtered between the buildings of downtown Eden. Uncle Hank had purchased and restored a brick building located in the town square, where small businesses surrounded the original courthouse. He walked into the office and grabbed the stack of mail from the reception desk. Getting Rebecca the job as the part-time librarian should have been a piece of cake. Why couldn't life be simpler?

Coffee. He needed coffee. He dropped the stack of bills on his assistant's desk and went to the break room to start a fresh pot. While it brewed, he made sure the conference room was ready for meetings he had with potential clients. He stopped at the conference table it was a family heirloom. It was made by a carpenter with space recessed into the table top and overlayed with clear glass. It allowed Uncle Hank to showcase pictures that chronicled the last one hundred years of Eden's history. Every time we sat down with customers they not only saw the history of the town but just how long our family had been in Eden.

He ran a calloused finger around the silhouette of the first Greystone man pictured in front of an old general store store. Uncle Hank hadn't come out and said it, but Walker understood that he had a chance to overcome the alcoholic reputations his father and grandfather left behind. He and his brothers could chart a different path.

He poured himself a cup of the freshly brewed coffee and sat behind the same scarred wood desk Uncle Hank and Wayne, Uncle Hank's father had used before him. His office windows faced the courthouse, giving him a perfect view of all the comings and goings of people he'd known his whole life.

He clicked open his calendar. Sometime today, he would find out if they were awarded the library contract.

The library.

Rebecca.

Vince's baby.

He gulped his coffee and scalded himself.

Just then, the back door opened, and the hollow sound of boots striding down the hall echoed through the office. So much for a quiet morning to collect his thoughts and prepare for his day.

Robert, his younger brother by four years, appeared holding a steaming coffee. He dropped into the chair in front of the desk.

"You're here early, bro. Rough night?" Robert questioned as he sipped his coffee.

"Couldn't sleep." Walker shuffled papers on the desk.

"You usually sleep like a rock. Something happen?" Robert propped his boots on the edge of the desk.

"I heard Aunt Bell puttering around the house last night and again early this morning. Then there's this whole thing with Rebecca."

Robert raised an eyebrow. "That's not unusual. We all know Bell is restless at night."

"Except I heard her in Vince's old room going through his

things. Crying," his brother told him. "And when I woke up, I realized she'd gone to the family plot. Again."

The coffee roiled in Walker's stomach. How could he fix her grief? First Uncle Hank and now Vince.

She was grieving.

They all were.

Except he was more angry than grief-stricken. Vince's death had been senseless. He'd been drinking and driving. Irresponsible.

Walker stood. "I need help preparing for today's job in the warehouse. Can you lend a hand?"

"Sure." Robert took a swig of his coffee as they walked from the offices to the warehouse in the back.

"I don't know about Rebecca being here." Robert said as he flipped on the lights in the warehouse.

Walker picked up clipboard on the back wall that held the pull sheet for today's job. "We need the five-ton condenser and air handler." He put the sheet back up and said to Robert, "You think that wasn't obvious after your comment Sunday?"

Robert grabbed the pallet jack and strode to the row of equipment."I didn't mean to hurt her feelings." Robert told him.

"Bell is over the moon happy about Vince's child. Too happy." Walker set the pallet jack under the condenser and pulled the handle to lift the equipment.

"That's bad?" Robert questioned.

"I don't know if it's bad. But I probably have the same questions and concerns that you do. What if Rebecca leaves after she has the baby? Where will that leave Bell?" Walker asked as he pulled the equipment to the staging area and dropped the jack, releasing the unit.

Robert ignored his comment and instead motioned him

over to the air handler. "Bell said Rebecca's lease was up on her apartment. Why didn't her family step in to help?"

Walker loaded the air handler onto the pallet jack and pushed it toward the staging area. "She doesn't have much family. At least I don't think. She mentioned her mother is dead, and her father lives in Trinidad. I know she has a great-aunt somewhere in New York and a few cousins." Walker ran up the stairs where the ductwork was stored and slid boxes down the shoot.

Robert grabbed each box of duct as they came down and set them next to the waiting equipment.

Walker stopped dropping duct and stood, one box next to him, forcing Robert to look up. "I have so many questions. Like, why didn't Vince tell us about the baby? If it weren't for her showing up here, we wouldn't have ever known. Vince is gone, and I'm more concerned about Aunt Bell than ever." Walker shoved the box down with force. "I mean, this is the last thing Bell needs right now." Walker stomped down the stairs and moved to the slab section. "What any of us needs."

Robert stacked the last of the boxes of ductwork and turned to him. "Vince was in a relationship with her for two years and if anyone should know what's going on, it's you. You were the only one Vince stayed in contact with after he moved to Houston."

"He didn't marry her, and he left no provision for the baby. You'd think he would've learned from what we went through with Mom dying, Dad taking off, leaving us with nothing and no one." Walker grabbed the slab and hefted it up in his arms and set it next to the equipment.

"Exactly my point, man. I don't think it had anything to do with Rebecca. He didn't want to settle down or stay in one place. Remember, that's why he took the sales job and left Eden. If you ask me? He was selfish and wanted to travel and be responsibility free. But the fact is, I'll never know the why of it and neither will you. This is the situation. We just need to help as best we can. But you should be asking yourself why you care so much." Robert faced him, eyebrows raised in question.

"How can you even ask that?" At Robert's shrug, he said, "I care because she's pregnant. I care because it's the right thing to do. Family takes care of family. Can you imagine if she left now? Bell would be devastated. We have to make sure she gets the job in town."

Shaking his head, Robert looked Walker in the eye. "You're doing it again."

"What?" Walker lifted his hands.

"Trying to save everyone."

Walker moved away and checked the pull sheet. "What are you talking about?"

Robert groaned. "Bro, you are not everyone's keeper."

Walker moved to the installation totes section. He wished he could distance himself from the entire conversation. But he couldn't. He hefted the fifty-pound tote and turned back to the staging area only to find Robert leaning against the condensing unit, arms folded. "I know you promised Mom, and you probably promised Hank too." At Walker's blank look, Robert shook his head. "To take care of us."

Walker froze. He hadn't told anyone. How did Robert know? He *had* promised Mom before the paramedics took her. It was the last time any of them had seen her alive after their parents fought. "Is that everything?" He motioned to the staging area.

Robert nodded. Walker headed back to his office. But the thump of Robert's boots behind him told him their conversation was not done.

Walker dropped into his office chair. The silence thickened as Robert did the same.

"You promised to take care of us, and you did that. But now it's time to let go. We're all grown up," Robert said.

Walker was the oldest and therefore responsible for his family. Age didn't matter.

"What happens if she doesn't get the librarian position?" Robert questioned as he tossed his empty coffee mug from hand to hand.

Let another woman down? He was still struggling to keep the promise he made all those years ago to his mother. Walker could not entertain failure with Rebecca. Would not.

"We'll figure out something." Robert shrugged. "Bell's been thinking about buying tiny houses, setting them up around our lake and starting a rental business. Maybe she can help Bell work on that."

"There's still a good chance she stays, has the baby and then leaves," Walker pressed. "That would destroy Bell."

Robert stopped tossing the mug back and forth. "When did you become so cynical?"

"I don't know. Watching Dad beat Mom, or becoming orphans might have done it." He snapped his fingers. "Or maybe it might be living in this town where even after two decades, people keep painting us with the same brush as our alcoholic, wife-beating, good-for-nothing father and grandfather."

Robert raised a brow. "You also spent the last decade in the same household as Hank and Bell. Did you see how much they loved one another? Doesn't that count for something?"

Doubt hovered in the dark recesses of Walker's mind. It was probably the reason why he was still single after all these years. He made a face. "They had a once-in-a-lifetime romance. That doesn't come along too often. I'm concerned about Bell, and I know you are too. She's fragile, and I don't want her heart broken again."

Robert leaned forward on his forearms. "Neither do I."

"Honestly, I know Vince is dead but I'm angry at him. He had everything we didn't. Loving parents, a great home and a legacy. And he threw it all away." Walker dropped his head.

"I agree, but we can't change the past. Let's focus on helping Bell. Be here for her, help her. She's not just sad that Vince is gone, but she's questioning herself."

"About what?" Walker frowned.

Robert pinched the bridge of his nose. "Every time Aunt Bell gets like this, she asks why Vince made the choices he did."

Walker cocked his head to one side. How had he missed this? "What do you say to her?"

Robert shrugged. "What can I say? He made his choices, and it isn't a reflection on her."

Walker ran his hands through his hair.

"Walker, she has *us*," Robert said, shifting in his chair.

"You know more than anyone else, grief isn't logical and doesn't have a time frame."

Robert stood. "Leave Miranda out of this."

Walker hadn't meant to bring up Robert's late wife, who died last year. He sighed. When would he learn?

Robert stalked toward the door and stopped. "You always have a plan, Walker. So, what's your plan this time?"

"Bell needs Rebecca and the baby as much as Rebecca and the baby need us. Let's focus on keeping her here and keeping her healthy."

Robert shifted, one foot out the door. "Those are a lot of things to focus on."

"Yeah, well, with the five of us, we just might be able to pull it off," Walker said.

Robert shot his brother a crooked grin. "You're going to need all the help you can get. Word's out the mayor is angling for Denise to get that job."

How had Robert heard about that already? The downfall of living in a small town was good news *and* bad news traveled faster than the speed of light.

"Don't remind me. Can you be positive about anything?" Walker grumbled.

Robert held up his empty cup. "Coffee's good."

Walker's email dinged on his phone. He reached for it, opened it to read the notification.

"We got it!" Walker shot to his feet and thrust a fist in the air.

"Got what, bro?" Robert asked.

"We got the library job!" He rounded the desk and fist-bumped his brother.

Stowing his phone in his back pocket, Walker reached for the landline. "I'm going to order the equipment. If they have it in stock, we can get a jump on the installation." Walker nodded toward his brother's now empty coffee mug. "Better grab another cup. It's going to be a busy week."

Walker's mind buzzed with excitement at the possibilities. This library job was a great opportunity for Greystone Home Services. Working with JC Construction would provide exposure for their business in the commercial market. Not to mention it would provide steady work during the slow months.

Now if Rebecca landed the library job, everything would be perfect. Right?

Tired of waiting for her phone to ring with news of the library job, Rebecca opened the sliding glass door to the back porch with her Bible and journal in hand. She needed to study the scriptures because she couldn't help but wonder if she'd traded one unemployed location for another. Her phone buzzed. She opened the text message, which said her bank account was below $300. Quickly she opened the bank app. Balance: $273.22. She set her phone face down and dropped into the porch swing. What were her options? How else could she save money? She'd stopped by the grocery store and purchased some necessities: peanut butter, honey, a loaf of bread, crackers, a carton of eggs, a gallon of milk, tea and a small pack of generic butter. She splurged on the flour and tomatoes to make the choka. She was thankful to be able to stay in this mini apartment attached to the house but she didn't want to intrude on the family. After all, they didn't even know about her before this week.

She took a sip of tea and tried to think of job options. The Texas heat was rising, but she enjoyed being outside too much to stay inside. This was something she'd always imagined she'd do with Vince and the baby. A house, a backyard, afternoons in the country, family picnics. Instead, she was alone.

She placed her Bible and journal on the end table. She'd seen the name of Bell's church on a magnet on the refrigerator and had watched the service streaming online. She hadn't been ready to face the entire family again. Pastor Jeff Dunn said God was a good father. But she was still trying to reconcile that idea. Her father had ignored her. Left her and her mother. Vince had done the same to her and the baby.

All her life she tried doing the right thing, focusing on studying and school, yet here she was. With a master's degree but unemployed. Alone and pregnant.

She'd given everything to her relationship with Vince, yet ultimately he hadn't wanted her or their baby.

She couldn't seem to keep people in her life. What was wrong with her?

She rubbed her belly. "Don't worry, little one. You are wanted and we *will* have a home together."

Suddenly her phone on the side table vibrated. She checked the screen.

Unknown number. Should she answer? She didn't want another scammy phone call, but what if it was a job she'd applied for?

She answered. "Hello?"

"Hi, is this Rebecca Young?"

"Yes, this is Rebecca."

"Hi, Rebecca, this is Beth Porter from the library."

"Oh, hi." Hope fluttered in her stomach.

"I wanted to thank you for taking the time to come in and talk to me earlier this week."

Here was the brush-off. At least she was getting one by phone instead of email.

"I checked your references, and they all had good things to say about you."

Her hand tightened on the cell. That was good, wasn't it? "Thank you."

"We'd like you to join our team. If you accept, we'd like to offer you the part-time position."

"I…" She could only stare unfocused. Had she heard correctly?

"Rebecca?"

Something *was* going to turn out right. For once.

She cleared her throat. "Yes, I'd love to."

"That's great to hear. I know you just moved to town, but when would you like to start? Not to pressure you, but the sooner, the better—the reading program is underway, and with the remodel, that requires we shuffle some sections around. We need all the help we can get."

"I can start tomorrow, if that works for you." She did a little happy dance in her chair.

"Great. I will see you tomorrow at 8:00 a.m., then."

"Thank you." She bit her lip in an attempt not to let the excitement leak out in her voice.

"You're welcome. We are eager to have you join our library team. See you tomorrow."

Rebecca pressed end on the cell and held it to her belly. "Hear that, little one? Mommy has a job." Her stomach suddenly bumped out. It might be her imagination, but she was sure he gave her a fist bump from within.

"Things are looking up. It's only part-time, but it's in your daddy's hometown, and, well, it looks like we finally landed in a good place."

At least she hoped so.

Chapter Six

Where had she gone wrong? Rebecca threw the last of the soaked towels into the garbage. She shook her hands over the trash. Great, a librarian with red hands.

What a way to start her second week on the job. She surveyed the decimated Activities Room. Decorated in a soothing gray with natural light streaming in from double pane windows and artwork displayed from the previous month's art contest, it was the perfect, roomy, yet cozy enough space for story time. Small plastic blue chairs were set in a semicircle.

The snack table in the back of the room was up against the wall. Story time had begun with fruit punch, cookies and cake on the table. She pulled off the white tablecloth, balled it up, stuffed it in the trash can as well.

"I hear there was a little excitement during story time today." Wearing his typical polo shirt and denim jeans, Walker strode in.

"I would say that is the understatement of the day." Rebecca reached for the broom and swept up the crumbs from under the gray plastic tables. She dumped the squashed cake into the garbage. Banging the dustpan against the rim of the large black trash bag, the icing stuck, but a discarded napkin got it off. If only she could brush off this day. "Maybe the understatement of the *year*."

"Want to tell me what happened?" Walker pushed the stack of chairs to the back wall closer to the storage closet.

"You mean you didn't get a play-by-play from Beth?"

Walker shook his head. "Oh, I heard, but I wanted to get the details from you."

How to explain today's epic failure? She put the remaining gallons of punch on the cart and dumped the half-eaten tray of cookies into the trash. She needed to tell him. After all, it was his reputation on the line since he vouched for her to get this job.

"You know a cute little boy, blue eyes, freckles, gap-toothed. Dresses in overalls and boots?"

Walker arched his eyebrow. "Tommy Coldwell started this?"

She slid onto an empty kid's chair. She rubbed her face before answering.

"Tommy was full of excitement when he got here, and I could see that his grandmother had her hands full with his younger brother while Tommy bounced everywhere. He went to the back of the room, the front of the room, and back again. Everywhere."

Walker motioned for her to continue.

"I thought if I kept him occupied, it would keep him busy and help his grandmother. I showed him how to make an airplane. It would keep his mind and hands engaged until story time started."

"And?"

"Instead, I weaponized him."

Walker grinned, his dimples showing. "Weaponized him?"

"Weaponized," she repeated.

He burst out laughing.

"You laugh, but it was pandemonium for ten minutes before I could get the kids under control." Rebecca slumped in the chair. "Maybe giving a five-year-old an airplane wasn't the brightest solution."

Walker cleared his throat, suppressing a smile. "I mean, you had good intentions. But maybe it wasn't the best idea."

"Oh, it wasn't." She massaged her temples. "It was the worst idea."

Head cocked, Walker asked, "So, what happened next?"

"He must be an expert plane thrower because before I knew it…" She raised her arm and imitated throwing the plane. "He decided it flew lopsided, so he took his gum out of his mouth and tried to even the weight in the wings."

"Tommy's one bright little boy. His father is an engineer."

Rebecca groaned. "That explains it, because his little airplane adjustment caused the plane to fly right into Mrs. Neilson's new hairdo. Before I knew it, Tommy ran up to where the plane landed in her hair." Rebecca motioned. "She was seated next to her granddaughter, in the last row. He tried to retrieve it, but the gum stuck, and when he pulled, she screamed and jerked forward. He fell back, grabbed the plastic table cloth, and down came the refreshment table. Which began Operation Red Sea." She waved her hands toward the semiclean room and the trash filled with red paper towels full of the spilled punch. "And that, my friend, was the end of story time."

"I guess we could say it wasn't a boring day." Walker continued to stack chairs next to her. "Hey, we all have bad days every once in a while."

Rebecca squeezed her eyes shut. In fact, she'd love to fast forward the day to dinner time with Bell. That was something she'd begun to enjoy about country living. The smell of the pine trees mixed with the sounds of the insects while she sat with a cup of tea on the back porch after dinner. Sometimes Bell stayed with her, sometimes she sat by herself. She sighed. So peaceful unlike this morning. She'd wanted to make a good impression with her first event. "I'll take boring. Any day of the week, in fact."

. She stood and helped him stack chairs.

Walker grinned. "I think this is where I say, it could've always been worse, but I'm not sure how."

"No kidding. Being a librarian is supposed to be quiet and steady. No craziness."

He blinked. "You're kidding, right? Story time with little kids that haven't learned to sit still?"

Rebecca grabbed the all-purpose cleaner and sprayed the table.

After she was done, Walker closed the table, hefted it and set it inside the storage closet in the back of the room.

"I mean, I expect some things to go wrong. But this?"

After he set the second table inside the storage closet, he said, "Stop, it was an unfortunate incident. Things happen. The most important thing is nobody was seriously hurt. And hey, you think this was chaotic?" Walker pointed to the room at large. "If you want to experience outrageous behavior, try the adult book club. Bell told me, Larry, the UPS guy threw his hat at Mr. O'Riley during the discussion. Boring? Ha! On second thought, maybe you shouldn't go tonight. I think you've had enough excitement for one day." Walker pushed the last stack of chairs into the storage room and closed the door.

Rebecca surveyed the results of her cleaning efforts. The linoleum floor was damp but clean, with no traces of the mess. She unlocked the wheels of the cart and stood by the door as Walker pulled out the trash liner and tied it into a knot.

"I talked to Beth. I have news. Well, it depends on how you look at it."

"Please tell me it's good news." Rebecca pushed the cart into the bright hallway where she could hear the steady beep of books being checked out and the muffled conversations of patrons.

"I found out through the wind-vine—"

She turned to Walker. "Wind-vine?"

Walker grimaced. "It's an Aunt Bell word. Wind-vine aka the grapevine. Word travels like the wind in this small town."

"Ah. Makes sense."

"Anyway, Lauren Stoker won't be returning once she has her babies."

"Lauren?"

"She's the other full-time librarian. She had to start her maternity leave early so I don't think you got a chance to meet her. She's carrying twins and on bed rest right now for the rest of her pregnancy."

"Okay." Rebecca's grip tightened on the cart. "Could it mean…"

Walker nodded, his grin irresistible. "Yes, there will be a full-time position open in September."

"You do know my baby is due around then?"

"Don't worry. I have a plan."

"You do?" Rebecca couldn't wait to hear what it was. From where she stood, this was an amazing opportunity. A full-time job in a small town. With benefits. Could things be finally looking up?

"Yes, but I have an ulterior motive."

Rebecca's hope quickly fizzled.

He didn't seem to notice. "The mayor scheduled the grand

reopening of the library the same day as the start of the Fair on the Square event."

"You mentioned he'd moved it up."

"He did. Beth is putting you in charge of special events for the day."

That was a big responsibility. "But—"

Walker held up his hand. "Today, you showed you could handle yourself under pressure. Plus, she was able to authorize another ten hours a week for this project. That gives you thirty hours a week."

Rebecca could only nod. She appreciated Walker's help. It'd been so long since she could depend on others. She let out a breath and smiled her thanks.

"It's not quite full time, but every little bit helps, right?" He winked, his blue eyes bright with hope. That wink, those dimples, they turned her insides to mush. She could feel her face heating up and her heart start to race. He was one good looking man, but more than that, she could see the goodness in him.

Walker stepped closer to her when a patron paused to review a book on a shelf near them.

"If you plan this successfully, I'm pretty sure you would get the full-time position. After all, the whole town will be watching." Walker headed toward the back door with the trash.

The whole town will be watching.

That was what she was afraid of. The whole town watching could be good or bad. Good, if she pulled this event off successfully. Bad, if she messed up the planning. She ignored the spark of fear. If today was any indication, bad could happen. She rubbed her belly as the little guy kicked. If she did this well though, she'd be one step closer to a full-time job, steady income and a good home life for him.

* * *

Rebecca took a deep breath. She could do this. She really could. There were a couple of months to plan. Beth had indeed handed the project to her.

Two hours later, papers covered every square inch of Rebecca's desk. She read Beth's ideas and created an action spreadsheet to ensure every single detail was captured. The re-opening of the library events would require finessing between the earlier date and their limited budget.

"Hi, Rebecca."

Bell stood in her doorway, wearing tan pants and a cream-colored shirt that had Book Nook embroidered on it.

"Hi, Bell, what are you doing here?"

"I'm volunteering today." Bell walked in and stood in front of her desk.

"Oh, that's right. I remember you telling me a while back. But I haven't seen you since I've been working here."

"I didn't want to make you nervous, so I switched with another volunteer, Rachel Stone. She loves books even more than I do. Besides," she whispered, "on Thursdays, we sort through all the donated books, and she gets first pick." She slipped a gift bag onto the desk. "A little birdie told me you loved this. I brought it here because I wanted you to have it while it was still warm."

Rebecca opened the bag. A loaf of banana bread was inside. Her mouth watered. Anything banana was appealing to her, but since getting pregnant, this was almost better than ice cream. Almost. "This is my favorite. Thank you." She set the loaf on the black metal desk.

"You're welcome." Bell wandered around her office. "I like how you've decorated."

Colorful pictures of places to visit—Hawaii, New Zealand, Alaska, and Finland—hung on the tan walls.

She could dream, couldn't she?

She and Vince had bonded over their shared love of travel, though she didn't seek adventure or escape like he had. She'd wanted to visit different places for the experience, but deep down, she'd wanted a home, a place to belong.

"I've barely seen Walker this week." Bell turned, her eyebrows raised in question. "Have you seen him?"

"I know he'll be here at some point. I don't always see him." She fumbled with the papers before her. The problem was she wanted to see him every day, but she shouldn't want to. She loved the way he'd stop and interact with a parent and child that were at the library. No matter how busy he was. Living at the ranch, she heard him leaving in the morning and returning late at night.

"Oh, I thought he might have stopped by to check in."

Rebecca shook her head but didn't make eye contact. "No." She wasn't going to mentioned he stopped by her desk every day to check in with her. Beth already picked up on his daily visits with her throughout the library.There was a matchmaking gleam in her eyes whenever she caught them talking. Rebecca was sure Walker was just being friendly. He even said he wanted to see how she was settling in.

Bell sighed, drawing her back to the present. "He's supposed to help me plan the activities for the grand opening. I promised Beth I would have the Book Nook volunteers man a booth."

Rebecca indicated the paperwork spread out before her. "That's what I'm working on right now. Beth put me in charge of the speakers and events."

The outer door opened, and an orange ladder clanked against the door frame.

Bell hurried out of Rebecca's office to hold the door open.

Walker appeared in her doorway, a Greystone Home Services ball cap shadowing his eyes. Wearing a company blue polo and work jeans, he leaned across the ten-foot ladder against the wall and kissed Bell on the cheek. "Hi, ladies."

Rebecca tried to focus on anything but the handsome Walker Greystone. She should be focused on work, on making this project a success. She wanted to thump her head on the desk. Why was she thinking about Walker? She was off relationships. Besides he was Vince's cousin, he should be the last person she should have feelings for. She was going to blame this temporary foolishness on pregnancy hormones.

"Hey Walker, we were just talking about you." Bell gave his arm a light squeeze.

He sniffed the air. "I'm sure you said, 'Oh, Walker will be at the library. I'll bring him my famous banana bread.'" He winked at Rebecca and nodded toward the bread on her desk.

Bell wagged her finger. "Now, young man, that loaf is for Rebecca. Don't you go trying to sneak a slice either."

He held up his hands. "Okay, okay. I won't try to steal a slice…while she's looking."

"Walker—"

"Just joking." He set the ladder up. "Rebecca, will it bother you if I work here? I've got to get up into the ceiling. I'll try to be as quiet as possible."

"No problem."

He leaned over to kiss his aunt again. "I gotta keep working."

Bell laid a hand on his shoulder. "Wait, we need to talk about the reopening of the library."

"What about it?" He slung his backpack of tools off his shoulder and set it on the floor.

Muscles bunched along his forearms as he moved. Rebecca shifted her eyes back to the papers strewn across her desk as heat rose up her neck. How would she concentrate with him working right outside her doorway? Should she be noticing things like that? He was Vince's cousin. A Greystone. No. She didn't need any entanglements—especially with someone related to Vince.

"Walker, since Beth put Rebecca in charge of the events, we can all work together. Won't that be fun?" Bell clapped her hands, beaming.

Rebecca reached for her water bottle. "Work together?"

Walker stood, screwdriver in his hand. "I'm not working on the grand opening, Aunt Bell. I'm working on the library HVAC."

Bell laughed. "Of course, you are. But we talked about this. You said you'd help me plan the booth for the Book Nook."

"Aunt Bell, I can't—"

She waved her hand. "We shouldn't talk about it while you are working anyway. I know you hate to be distracted." Bell scooted toward the door. "Don't worry, we can discuss it tonight back at the house. Enjoy the banana bread, Rebecca."

Walker stared at Bell's retreating back. "Somehow, I think she roped me in."

Rebecca grinned. "Yep, she did. Quite smoothly, I might add."

His phone vibrated. He pulled it off his belt clip and answered. "Yeah… I'm on my way." He dropped the tools into the backpack and looked at Rebecca. "They need me on the roof. I'll be right back."

After he hustled out the door, Rebecca stared at the banana bread. Maybe she could have one slice. No, if she gave in now, she'd end up eating all of it. Better to wait. She set it on the chair away from her desk. The farther away temptation was, the better.

Her gaze slid to the abandoned ladder and backpack near the doorway.

Today, she needed to try harder to resist her feelings about Walker Greystone, a man who exemplified all the qualities she wanted in a husband. She couldn't help but notice the way he treated Bell and his brothers, that Walker exemplified the family commitment she dreamed of for herself and her little one.

But she clearly wasn't meant to have a family of her own. That much was clear. She'd just keep everyone at arm's length till the little one came. Then she'd have to reassess. She wouldn't fool herself into believing she had a place with this family.

When Walker pushed open the library's back door, the sun almost blinded him. He adjusted his cap as he climbed the built-in ladder on the rear side of the building. Even if Aunt Bell manipulated him into helping on the project, he wanted to work with Rebecca. He enjoyed spending time with her. His daily stops at her desk were starting to be the highlight of his days.

"Walker, we got problems," his foreman called over the parapet.

"Coming." He scrambled up the remaining steps and wiped the sweat from his forehead as he reached the top of the building. Texas and humidity were great things for air-conditioning contractors. But problems, he could do without.

He strode to where Ricky Conner, Kenneth Stevens and Waylon Richards stood, feet braced apart, surrounding the commercial package unit. They wore similar aggravated expressions. Ricky was the old-timer of the group, his beard more salt than pepper. Dressed in khaki pants, with their company royal blue uniform shirt stretched over his belly, he scratched his bald head before setting the cap back.

"What's up, Ricky?"

"It's the wrong voltage," he said.

"What do you mean it's the wrong voltage?"

They couldn't afford any delays. Not with the moved-up timeline. The supplier already was one unit short as it was. This job had to go perfectly for him to convince JC Construction he should be the HVAC contractor for all of their jobs. If he didn't expand the business, it couldn't support his brothers and they would go elsewhere to find work. Which would leave Aunt Bell all by herself. This job had to go well.

"Hey! Y'all done up there? Clock's a tickin'," the crane operator yelled from below.

The wrong voltage meant they'd have to take this unit back down and return it to the vendor. "Ricky, explain the situation to the operator. I'll get on the phone with our vendor and see when we can get a replacement."

Walker found out that an additional unit wouldn't be available until September. But he'd promised the mayor, JC Construction, the committee and the whole town that this job would completed for the projected re-opening at the end of September.

Yet he'd come up short.

Just like his father. He detested the grip the past had on him. Every time he stepped off the ranch, he had to prove himself. No matter what he did or how hard he tried, his father's reputation shadowed his every move.

Chapter Seven

Walker entered Bakers hardware store to purchase a replacement socket set. Inside he was greeted by the steady hum of conversation. Chuck Brandon stood at the end of the aisle in his signature blue overalls and checkered shirt with Milton Rogers. They could be twins if it weren't for the fact one stood at 6'2" and the other at 5'2". They were dressed in their work uniforms of cowboy hats, work overalls, with cowboy boots. Those two had the most kind hearts he'd ever seen. If some project needed to be done at the church, they were the first to volunteer. He nodded to them as he continued into the store. The smell of fresh wood, fertilizer and sawdust melded together as he turned to the tool aisle. It was here, two weeks after his mother's funeral, that his maternal grandfather, spewing brandy fumes, had demanded custody of him and his brothers from Uncle Hank. He rubbed his left arm, the same arm his grandfather had grabbed. He shook off the memory and selected a socket set. He would be forever grateful that Uncle Hank stood up to his own father and kept them.

His phone buzzed. Glad for interruption, he slid open the screen. Kenny texted, Can you pick up tan caulk? Mrs. Needleston asked me to recaulk the baseboards in her craft room.

Walker replied, Caulking baseboards? When did we put that in an AC technician's job description?

You didn't know? he texted back. It's built into the DNA of any child raised in Eden, Texas. If they ask, you say yes ma'am. Just ask your aunt.

He chuckled as he sent him a thumbs-up emoji. Kenny was right. He went down two more aisles, found the caulk and picked up three tubes.

He nodded to Mr. Baker, the store manager, as he refilled the nail bins. The clink of the nails echoed as he passed Johnny Peter operating the key cutting machine. The young kid blew the metal filing off the key as Walker dodged the next person in the key line and headed to the checkout.

The old-timers were still in front of the store. Marvin Tucker, who could be mistaken for Santa Claus any time of the year, and Jimmy Fredricks, who topped six foot five with a mop of gray hair. That, combined with his foot-long salt-and-pepper beard, made people look twice. The men congregated around the coffee-pot every morning and had been doing so every day for the last ten years. It was local legend that the old-timers knew everything that happened in Eden. Often before the people being gossiped about knew.

Marvin's belly shook with laughter while Jimmy poured himself another cup of black coffee.

Walker scrolled through his emails while he waited in line to pay. If he had his choice, he would have chosen a different store. Baker's Hardware was more expensive, but it was local—old gossip never died here.

"Good morning, Gwen." Walker set his purchases on the counter in front of the cashier.

Gwen Richards hadn't aged a day since high school. Today she wore her bright red hair in a bun on top of her head.

Smiling, she picked up the first tube.

"Hey, I heard the new librarian is staying at the ranch."
Walker nodded.

"George told me he had fun at story time the other day."
Gwen passed the caulk across the scanner to ring up the price.

"Ahh, he enjoyed the flying plane show?" Walker slid his credit card out of his wallet and grinned. "I bet he helped himself to the extra cookies flying around."

Gwen pulled open a plastic bag as she bagged the caulk. "Knowing my boy, he gobbled up as many as he could. The poor new librarian, can you imagine that happening at your new job?"

Walker shook his head. "I can't. You know what horrors we were as kids."

"We were all terrors." Gwen smiled. "Mrs. Robin still shudders when I walk in the library with my kids."

Gwen scanned the socket set. "She's a real trooper, though. I would have quit or at least canceled future story time sessions. But not her. I received an email about the next event this morning. She's calling it 'Outer Space.'" Gwen bagged up the miscellaneous batteries he'd thrown in while waiting. "That is one brave woman."

Walker smiled at that statement. He agreed with Gwen; Rebecca was brave, she just didn't realize it. He admired her for that. When everything in life had gone wrong, she hadn't given up.

"Morning, Walker," bellowed Jimmy from the front of the store.

Walker glanced over his right shoulder at the men and gave them a stiff nod. "Morning, Jimmy. Marvin." Interesting. Jimmy usually never greeted him. In fact, he went to great pains to ignore Walker's existence.

"I heard you got the library job." Jimmy pointed a bony finger at him before he took a gulp of coffee.

"Yes, sir."

"Seems like a big job for a small outfit like yours."

"We can handle it."

"Yeah? I remember a few years back your dad took on the job for this store."

The screech of the key machine stopped. Just in time for everyone to hear the accusation in Jimmy's words.

"Did he? I didn't realize."

Jimmy pointed. "That's just it. He didn't. He got the job, took the down payment and didn't finish."

Silence fell over the store.

Walker turned and said, "Have a good day, Gwen."

Walker reached for the plastic bag and faced Jimmy. "Thanks for letting me know. But it's been, what, at least twenty years since that happened? And I'm not my father."

After twenty years why was he still fighting his father's reputation? It was a wonder that any of the Greystone brothers grew up to be successful with their father's failures constantly hanging over them.

Jimmy narrowed his eyes. "Let's hope so. You Greystones haven't lived up to your word in these here parts."

Marvin, standing next to Jimmy, shifted from one foot to another, his cheeks a rosy red. "Come on, Jimmy. Give the boy a break. Just because your nephew didn't get the job, don't take it out on him."

Jimmy jerked his head, his face red. He didn't like being called out in public. Walker didn't either. "This has nothing to do with that."

Walker glanced behind him. Not one customer had left the store since this conversation started.

He strode to the door, then paused. "Jimmy, *this* Greystone keeps his word. Don't judge me by my father or grandfather."

Jimmy smoothed down his beard. "Don't worry, we'll be watching."

No doubt.

Walker stalked toward his pickup. He threw the bag on his front seat and drove to the library.

He would prove to this town—and maybe to himself—he wasn't his father.

He kept his promises.

He parked in the back of the library and jerked his forty-pound tool bag from the cab of his truck and headed to the ladder.

Walker adjusted the backpack—he was used to carrying extra weight.

Every single day of his life.

Rebecca needed some fresh air, a break from all the empty spots she had to fill in the schedule for the week of events to kick off the reopening of the library after the remodel. The problem was she didn't know what kind of events to schedule. She was used to city life and out here people did things differently. She needed ideas. The update report on the opening schedule of events was due in two days, and she wasn't nearly ready. Eating lunch outside would be a welcome relief. The fragrant smell of honeysuckle followed her as she headed to the pavilion. She found an empty green park bench where the sun peeked through the leaves of the oak tree. Several birds with brilliant blue and red markings hopped around as an elderly man scattered bird seeds around his feet from his park bench. She opened her lunch kit and pulled out a turkey sandwich. She couldn't help but notice a lone bird stayed behind, pecking at the few leftover seeds on the ground.

While she ate, she scrolled through social media on her phone. Her college classmates had posted pictures of themselves at their new full-time librarian positions. While she prayed for a full-time position, she was grateful for the part-time job here in town. Beyond thankful that she'd landed here despite her past with Vince. She slid the app closed on her phone and opened her notes for the grand opening on her tablet.

Her cursor hovered under the blank for author speaker. What kind of author could she invite to read at the event? Did this town have any local authors? And if they did, what did they write?

Her phone, turned face down next to her tablet, buzzed.

She tapped her earbuds to answer, her eyes still on her notes. "Hello?"

"Rebecca?"

Auntie Grace.

Rebecca could kick herself. Why did she answer her phone without looking? She'd been dodging Auntie's calls for the past two weeks.

She forced a modicum of happiness into her voice. "Hi, Auntie!"

"Don't you, 'Hi, Auntie' me,' young lady! I've left messages on your phone three times in the last few weeks and no answer."

"I'm sorry, Auntie, I, um, was b—"

"Do you want to make an old woman sick with worry?"

Rebecca snorted. She couldn't help it. At five feet tall, Auntie Grace was Chinese, born and raised in Trinidad, along with Rebecca's father. Auntie talked fast, walked fast and didn't believe in boundaries. She was the nosiest, bossiest, bestest auntie. At least when someone wasn't attempting to keep secrets from her.

"Are you laughing at me?" she demanded, indignation oozing through the phone.

"Only because you called yourself old. We both know you aren't." Rebecca could imagine her auntie's grin.

"Never mind that, why haven't you called? What have you been doing? Did you find a job?"

That was Aunt Grace. Rapid-fire questions. No breath in between sentences.

"As a matter of fact, I did find a job." Rebecca flattened the empty bag of Cheetos. Folded it in half and then in half again.

"What? When? Is it in a safe area? Houston is not known as the safest city."

"Oh, Auntie Grace, like New York is?" Rebecca threw the empty bag into her lunch kit.

"Humph. Mind your manners, young lady. I've been navigating these streets just fine since I left Trinidad. Tell me about this job. And sit up straight."

How did Auntie know she was slouching? Rebecca sat up straight. "It's a part-time job at a library in Eden, Texas."

"You took a part-time job? How can you survive on a part-time job, and why? You have your degree." Her aunt's voice rose.

Rebecca rubbed her belly as her little guy kicked. "I'm hoping it doesn't stay part-time for long. If I do a good job on an upcoming project, I could get a full-time position."

No matter how much she longed to share about the baby, Rebecca couldn't tell her auntie that she was pregnant. Being a first-generation American, the pressure to be successful was enormous. Success did not include being unmarried and pregnant.

She wasn't ready to jump that hurdle today.

"I needed to get away from the city."

"Well, that's a good thing. Where is Eden? Is it safe?"

"It is. It's a small town in the piney woods of Texas."

"Where are you living?"

"On a ranch." Oof, that was a close one.

"A ranch?" Aunt Grace asked.

"My room faces a huge spring-fed pond. It's beautiful."

"Why does that town sound familiar?"

Appetite gone, Rebecca wrapped the rest of her sandwich and stuffed it in her lunch bag. Auntie would put the pieces together.

"Isn't that where your ex, Vince, was from?" Aunt Grace asked.

She zipped her lunch kit shut. "Good memory, Auntie."

"Why would you go there of all places?"

"It's a job, Auntie." Besides, unemployed pregnant women couldn't be choosey. But she couldn't tell Auntie that. Rebecca closed her eyes. A breeze blew through the trees, brushing through her hair and cooling her heated face.

"It's beautiful out here. You should come to visit." Offering was safe because she knew Auntie wouldn't leave New York.

"You know, I was just thinking that I could use a change of scenery. I think I will take you up on that offer. I would love to visit your little town of Eden".

Rebecca thought she might be ill. Auntie couldn't come to Eden.

"Hello? Rebecca? You still there?"

"I would love to have you visit, Auntie. It's a lovely place. Right now, I'm sitting in the park under an old oak tree. You would love it." Rebecca drained the last of her water from the bottle.

"That does sound lovely."

"Let me know when's a good time for you to visit. Can't wait to see you! Gotta run."

Rebecca stood and tossed the bottle into the recycle receptacle.

"I need to hear from you once a week, young lady."

"Yes, Auntie."

"Love you." Auntie blew a kiss to her over the phone.

"I love you too, Auntie." She smiled despite her stomach feeling woozy. Rebecca tapped the End button on her phone. How could she delay her aunt's arrival in town? If Auntie came to Eden, she'd find out about her pregnancy, and while she had to come clean about it some time, she didn't want to do it now.

Rebecca slid her phone and tablet into her purse and gathered the rest of her things. She passed a family picnicking. The husband and wife held hands across the picnic table while their two children munched happily beside them.

Would she ever have that? A loving husband? And why did the image of Walker pop up in her mind?

Chapter Eight

Rebecca tried to quell her nerves as she studied the empty schedule on her tablet. Rebecca's preliminary report of the library reopening events was due to Beth at the end of the day, and she wasn't near ready.

Multiple advertising samples, social media drafts and a vendor list lay scattered across the six-foot gray library table-top. Rebecca straightened each pile. She'd taken over one of the library study rooms because she needed space to work. Here, it was quiet and there was a whiteboard that spanned the width of the room. She needed to focus. Too much was at stake. She had to plan a week full of activities that would culminate with the start of the town's Fair on the Square. She let out a ragged breath.

Then she rubbed her belly. Her baby's future depended on this. She couldn't afford to mess this up. The whiteboard needed to be full of activities and despite her best efforts, it held too many blank space. Kind of like the empty spaces in her life right now. Rebecca used the marker to write the ideas she'd gathered so far.

All the ideas seemed too dull or too average. They lacked originality. The few vendors that had signed up were artisans who made things like custom leather bags, special homemade jellies, candles, and specialty wood items.

"Knock, knock." Walker poked his head in the room.

"Hey!" Walker, in his company blue polo shirt, braced his shoulder on the door frame. His smile. Those dimples. She felt herself blushing as she tucked her hair behind her ear. She should have taken more time with her appearance this morning.

"Hey. What are you doing here?"

"I need a reason to visit my favorite librarian?" He tilted his chin toward the board behind her. "Brainstorming for the big week?"

Trying to ignore that he called her his favorite librarian, she looked at the whiteboard. "Trying to. Every idea seems average and boring."

"Want some help?"

"Yes, please." She wasn't the kind of person to ask for help, but if Walker was offering, she wouldn't turn him down. Especially if it meant being with him for a few minutes. She hadn't seen him as often as she'd like since he was plenty busy with the library HVAC project. She'd take as much of his time—and presence—as he was willing to offer.

He closed the door behind him, grabbed a metal chair from the table and straddled it. "Let's see what you have scheduled so far."

She stepped to the side so he could read the entire board.

"Monday is Muffins with Moms at 9:00 a.m. and Tuesday will be Doughnuts with Dad at 10:00 a.m. Not bad for a start."

She blinked at the compliment, warmth flowing through her at his approval. "Just the basic activities. I heard the Fair on the Square events bring in a lot of people from surrounding areas. Truthfully, I don't see how anyone is going to want to come to the library when there are the fair attractions."

"Fair on the Square starts Saturday, not Friday. Don't

worry. You won't be competing for attendance. On Friday, the vendors set up their craft and food booths. Fair on the Square is coordinated by the Chamber of Commerce." He picked up an orange marker and twisted it around his fingers. He pointed to Friday's open space on her chart. "We can ask them to link and advertise our event along with theirs. But for now, let's focus advertising toward the locals."

"But what other activities can we offer?" She braced her hands on the back of the cold metal chair. "I have the normal things, but nothing that would attract people to come out after a busy workweek."

"Since the goal is family engagement, how about I talk to Mr. Brown and ask if he can bring his farm animals for a petting zoo on the Friday of the event?"

"Oh, the kids will love that!" She wrote Petting Zoo on the board. "Do you think we can interest the food trucks in serving lunch that day?"

"Sure, we can ask the food trucks already signed up for Fair on the Square. I'm sure they'd love the opportunity to sell more since they'll be here already. We can ask them to serve candied apples, kettle corn, burgers and hot dogs."

She jotted that idea on the board. "Maybe we can have food trucks for dinner too?"

Walker rubbed his chin. "Yes, that would be an incentive for nonlocals to drive up for a weekend getaway. Great idea!"

"Aunt Bell suggested we have refreshments that week. She mentioned letting the community know who was baking. More of a chance to have the community come out with the 'Best of the Best' bakers providing refreshments. We have a book sale that day too."

Walker pulled his phone from his back pocket. "Let me text some of the people I know."

Rebecca pointed the marker at Walker. "You know, I heard

Ms. Jennie makes the best strawberry cake. What if we added a baking competition?"

He grinned and snapped his fingers. "That's brilliant. You can have a local bake sale and a baking contest! You can ask Ms. Jennie to make her strawberry cake, Ms. Eleanor to make her famous lemon meringue pie and Aunt Bell to make her apple pie. I promise you, they will say yes."

"Really?" She scribbled their names under Bake Sale in her notebook.

"It's a matter of pride for them. Once word gets out there's a baking competition, you won't have problems with attendance. They'll come out for the dessert alone. Oh, and the Two Blondes Diner just opened adjacent to the courthouse. Their food?" He kissed his fingers. "Life-changing."

She underlined the caption that read Library Daily Activity. "I want to plan activities inside the library during the day as well. Right now, we only have the two activities."

"I thought you were going to get an author to do a reading?" Walker asked.

"I tried getting in touch with several authors but haven't heard back."

He stood and paced back and forth. "What about Fayetteville? Ms. Dee, who used to teach Sunday school, moved to Fayetteville to be closer to her kids." Walker turned his phone toward Rebecca. Colorful children's books filled the screen. "Dee writes children's books. She's also traveled extensively, so her books are multicultural. Then there's Ms. Shirley, who used to run a missionary children's school in Kenya. She's got a new children's book out too."

"And they were both local at one time?"

He nodded, his fingers tapping on his phone.

"That would be great. How do I get in touch with them?"

A flicker of hope ignited in Rebecca's chest. Just maybe, with Walker's help, she could actually do this.

"I'm sending you Dee's contact info right now."

Her phone pinged and she reached for it, nodding. "Got it."

Walker cleared his throat. "You might not want to mention our connection. She's still shuddering from the last prank my brothers and I pulled when she retired from Sunday school."

Rebecca lasered in on his nonchalant expression. "Walker, what did you do?"

He grinned, his dimples out in full force. "Come on, why did you assume it was me?"

She snorted. "You just said your brothers and you…"

Walker held up his hands. "I misspoke. It wasn't me. It was Parks. He slipped our pet mouse into her handbag."

Rebecca shuddered. "No, you didn't."

"I didn't. Parks did. Uncle Hank grounded us for a month." He tried to look contrite, but the twinkle in his eyes ruined the attempt.

"That poor lady."

He waved his hand at her. "Nah, she got us back. Decided not to retire till the next year, and I became her 'helper' for the rest of the term."

Rebecca bit the end of her pen, desperately trying to hold in laughter. "That doesn't sound all bad."

His mouth twitched. "Yeah, tell that to my younger self. Staying after church to clean up when everyone else was on the playground was not fun."

"I bet Bell made sure you were early too."

"Oh yeah." He nodded.

"Why would you bring a pet mouse to church?"

"It just sort of happened. Parks brought the mouse to church. When we got there, he couldn't keep it in his pocket, so he slipped it into Ms. Dee's handbag. You know how church ladies are." He stretched his hands. "Their bags are like suitcases. Parks figured the mouse would have room to play. He didn't count on her using her bag while in class. She reached for the lesson plan, and it crawled up her arm."

"Oh, no." Rebecca suppressed a shudder and rubbed her arms. "You got to be her 'helper'. What about Parks?"

He shook his head. "It was just me."

"But your brother did it."

"I was the older one, though. It was my job to keep an eye on him."

Rebecca tucked her hair behind her ear. She couldn't help but think that even then, he was responsible. Why hadn't she fallen in love with someone like Walker? Instead, she'd picked Wanderlust Vince. She couldn't help but wish she'd made better choices.

He braced his hands on the back of the metal folding chair. "I can contact some friends and ask about other booths."

"If you give me their contact information, I can call them. I know you have a lot going on." She nodded to the almost full whiteboard. "I have a rough schedule lined out for the days and now the night."

"What about a local adult author? Add in a giveaway— it could be the big finale. It would also help get people here on Friday night."

Rebecca wrote Giveaway on the whiteboard. "You know, you might have something there. Beth mentioned a local author who wrote a children's series using our library in one of her books, and it was popular. I don't remember the name, though."

"I know it. I went to school with Tagg. If you can tear her away from her day job, she'd probably do it. You should talk to Aunt Bell, though. I don't have her number, but Aunt Bell would."

"Wait, Tagg, as in Lisa Tagg?" She screeched and clapped her hands. "Walker! I love her children's books! She's from here?"

He shrugged. "Yeah."

"Walker, that's awesome. Plus, if she's from here, people will love to see one of their own being successful."

"I guess. I mean, to me she's just our postman's daughter."

She added Lisa Tagg's name next to Dee's and Shirley's. A dozen more booths and activities had been added. She stepped back from the whiteboard. "Thank you, Walker, you really helped a lot."

"Nah, just gave you some ideas. You get to do the real work."

"What do you mean?" She pointed to the whiteboard. "This was work."

"No, the real work comes in coordinating things, arranging the booths, fixing the times for set up and take down, working with the local police department to cordon off streets. Not to mention getting advertising for the event. Then there's getting Beth to let loose the budget. Have fun with that one. That lady's husband is a CPA, and he's taught her to make a dollar stretch pretty far." He stood up and tucked the chair back under the table. "Good luck."

"Thanks again."

He headed to the door. "Oh, and Aunt Bell would like you to come out to dinner with us tomorrow. We are celebrating the library contract by going to her favorite Italian restaurant."

"Just Aunt Bell?" Where had that come from? She could feel the blush as it stole up her neck.

Walker paused in the doorway as a slow smile stretched across his face. "Not just Aunt Bell. I'd like you there too."

Her pulse jumped as she took in his words. He wanted her there too.

It had been a long time since she belonged anywhere. Dinner was a good place to start.

Rebecca needed to get her mind off the fact that the speakers she'd emailed requests to had refused. She bent down to pull a dusty box from the bottom shelf in the gray storeroom. Who knew the library kept so much stuff besides books? When Beth mentioned this room needed to be organized, to make room for another shift in the library due to the remodel, she volunteered.

Anything to pass the time until she received a response from the authors she'd invited to speak. Beth had accepted her schedule of events but wanted confirmations as soon as possible. A week had passed, and only half a dozen vendors confirmed attendance. But still no answer from the other special speakers she'd requested. Zip. Nada. No responses.

Rebecca hefted the box onto the worktable and dusted her hands off. After talking with Bell, the local radio station agreed to emcee their main event Friday. That was the one good thing so far.

She tried to read the label on the outside of the box, but it was too faded. She opened the lid and peered at the hodgepodge of items inside. Oh, yeah, definitely, circa 1980. She pulled out an old action figure that looked like a bodybuilder. She laughed as she moved his gigantic biceps arm up and down. Why was this even in the box? Perhaps a kid left it behind?

Rebecca tossed the action figure into the trash, reached for dusty and faded crafts, and added them to the rubbish pile.

She needed a moment to regain her equilibrium after dodging the mayor's call. He wanted the speaker lineup for the week, but she didn't have one yet. And she didn't want to give them a reason to fire her and hire Denise.

"All three of them said yes!" Bell exclaimed as she swept into the room.

"What? When?" Rebecca answered. At Bell's quick nod, Rebecca rocked back on her shoes, stifling the urge to do a happy dance around the table.

"I knew there might be room on Ms. Dee's schedule and even Mrs. Shirley's, but how did you get Lisa Tagg to agree? When I called and asked if she was available her agent said she was booked through next year," Rebecca said.

"I just asked and then I prayed and prayed some more." Bell shrugged. "Sometimes God answers when you least expect it."

She tightened her hands and pumped a fist in the air. "Finally!"

Bell laughed and hugged her. "Rebecca, I don't know why you're so surprised."

She threw out her hands. "I've been waiting days to get a response from everyone and nada. Nothing. I have so much riding on this event, it's making me twitchy."

"I have complete confidence in you, Rebecca. Give yourself a little credit."

She let her hair fall to cover her face as her eyes started filling with tears. Was she that starved for approval that the slightest show of support got her all teary-eyed?

For some reason, she stood a little taller. Things were looking up. Now all she needed was to get more vendors to sign up and she might just pull off the best library grand reopening this town ever experienced. She couldn't wait to tell Walker.

More and more she realized that she wanted to spend time with him, and that was courting trouble she didn't need.

Chapter Nine

Today was the big day. He had to finish the library job in time for the grand reopening. His reputation and the reputation of Greystone Home Services was at stake. The crane had arrived to set the AC unit on the roof of the building, but the weather conditions weren't helping his confidence. The winds ripped through the trees as the crane navigated toward the back of the library. They were in hurricane season, and one had already entered the Gulf. Eden was already feeling the effects of the incoming storm. But there was no way he could reschedule the crane—they were already behind schedule.

The crane operator, a man with gray-and-white whiskers wearing a black veteran baseball cap, jumped out the cab and offered his hand. "You the boss man?"

Walker shook his hand. "I'm Walker Greystone."

"I'm Ben Krenek." The operator rubbed his bristled chin and looked at the empty alleyway between the buildings. The odor of four-day-old trash in the shared old rusted green dumpster lingered despite the windy conditions. "It's going to be touch-and-go with all this wind. Sure you want to do this?"

A forgotten newspaper blew toward them, only to get caught in the prickly bushes. Walker checked the weather app. He had until 4:00 p.m. today to get this unit up and running before the rain hit. "We're behind schedule. Since we won't see rain for another four hours, now's our one shot before the thunderstorms move in."

The older man removed his beat-up cap, scratched his head and stretched his neck to look up at the roof. "It's going to be tricky, but we can give it a shot." He tapped the screen on his tablet and handed it to Walker. "Here's the work order. Please sign, authorizing the work and the release of liability."

Walker offered up a quick prayer for safety as he scrawled his finger over the signature line.

He held his breath as the crane began to lift the unit. Midway up, wind tunneled between the buildings causing the fifteen-ton unit to sway between the power lines and the building.

Walker gripped the edge of the truck bed as the unit came dangerously close to hitting the brick building.

The operator paused the crane as another gust of wind blew between the buildings.

Walker sprinted toward the roof ladder and climbed to the rooftop.

The operator started moving the unit as another gust billowed through. The unit swung away from the brick, gained momentum and crashed into the four-foot ledge. Bricks cascaded down the side of the building and crashed to the concrete below, leaving a huge jagged hole. Walker froze and braced himself against the ladder. His throat tightened as the reality of the building damage set in. His gut twisted as he surveyed the destruction below.

The operator stopped and yelled, "Everyone all right?"

Though he wasn't, Walker still gave a thumbs-up and rushed the rest of the way up the ladder.

The operator proceeded to move the package unit into

place. Walker stepped next to the technician, Ricky, while the installers, Waylon and Kenneth, stood on the other side. The unit clanked into place with a dull thud. Walker removed the crane hook and signaled Ben. The operator swung the now empty hook to the edge of the building and back down.

Walker nodded to Ricky, and the crew started connecting the unit.

He scraped his hand over his face as he walked over to the jagged edge of the wall, staring at the scattered broken bricks below.

Ricky joined him, wiping his sweaty face with a towel. "I wouldn't want to be you today, boss."

Walker gripped the back of his neck. "Yeah, I don't particularly want to be me right now either."

The side door of the library banged open. Walker peered over the broken brick wall as the mayor and town reporter ran out.

Great, just great.

Mayor Stephenson shouted, "Walker, what happened?"

Next to him stood the local reporter, followed by John Beckman, the owner of JC Construction. The reporter wasted no time, his face hidden by the camera as he took shots of the scattered bricks, the crane operator, the crane and finally Walker.

Walker stepped back from the ledge.

Ricky clapped him on the shoulder. "Looks like you're up."

Walker felt the pressure of a job gone wrong balloon in his chest but he forced himself to head back down the roof ladder as the wind shifted yet again, the clouds moving at a furious pace across the darkened sky.

Wonderful. Seems like the mayor, a reporter, and his

boss, John, all had front-row seats to another Greystone mess up. Could the day get any worse?

How was Walker going to fix the damage to the building? This accident would add weeks to his timeline for completion. Forget any profit from this job. He'd paid extra to get the unit rushed here, now this. He could say goodbye to the service van he desperately needed to replace the one that kept breaking down.

Before he could address John Beckman, the mayor demanded, "What happened?" He stood with his hands on his hips, his complexion a shade of red.

Heat ran up Walker's neck to his face. "Mayor Stephenson, I… I'm—"

The mayor stared at the pile of cracked bricks before them. "I asked you a question, Walker. What happened here?"

James Black, the local reporter, stood there taking more photos, the whir of the camera loud in his ears as he stood before the mayor. Another Greystone failure in Eden front and center.

Just then, the winds stopped, and the sun broke through, illuminating the cloud of dust drifting over the cracked bricks littered across the alleyway. He'd started the day with high hopes. But this was turning into a nightmare. He braced his legs apart. "Strong winds caused the unit to sway right before we set it in place. The unit bumped against the parapet wall."

"Bumped?" Mayor Stephenson pointed to the gaping hole in the top of the building. "It looks like he took a bulldozer to the building."

They all looked up.

"It hit more than the parapet wall—I see damage below it," the mayor stated.

Walker could only nod, his throat dry as the dust continued to billow around their feet. It was obvious from the mayor's glare that he expected an answer. He cleared his throat. "We'll fix it." He didn't know how, but he would find a way.

Mayor Stephenson pointed his finger at him. "You had better. This building was one of the first dozen brick buildings built in Texas in the mid-1800s."

Walker shifted his feet from left to right.

The mayor loosened his tie and paced back and forth. "This cannot be happening."

The sound of murmuring voices made him turn. A group of people gathered at the front of the alley.

He ran his hands through his hair and tried to maintain a professional facade, but inside he was anything but. A red-and-blue service uniform caught his eye. Of course, Jimmy's nephew, Don, would be here. Jimmy from the hardware store would hear about this in no time. Don stood, arms crossed with a grin from ear to ear. The reporter, not done taking pictures, panned the crowd and took a shot. Great.

The mayor paced in front of the pile of scattered bricks. He jabbed his finger toward the debris. "You fix this, and it better not delay the reopening. I don't have to tell you how bad this would be publicity-wise for your company."

Walker winced as the noise from the crowd grew. The damage was done. Bad publicity was already in the works.

Mayor Stephenson stomped away, muttering to himself.

John Beckman reminded him of an old-time cowboy. He wasn't just the owner of JC Construction, but owned one of the largest spreads around Eden. From his tan Stetson to his long sleeved flannel shirt, starched jeans and weathered boots, he walked and spoke old-time cowboy. Here, on this job site, he was Walker's boss. And the boss wasn't happy. John tipped back his Stetson and crossed his arms. "Walker, I took a chance using your company. I expect you to make this right or you can forget about working with my company again. If you can't fix this, I will be hiring another HVAC company to finish the job."

He nodded. "Understood. I will take care of this." He didn't know how, but he would.

"And I expect this job to be finished on time. No delays." John pointed his finger toward Walker.

"Yes, sir."

After John left, Walker turned to the broken bricks and exhaled. The click of the camera drew his attention. More photos. Walker nudged a cracked brick at his feet.

Narrowing his eyes on James, the reporter for the paper, he asked, "Is there any chance you'd keep this out of the paper?"

"No way. It's my duty to report this to the citizens of Eden. I can help you out though and give you the headline. 'Local contractor destroys town library.'"

"Come on, James, that's not what happened here."

James shrugged before taking a few last photos and left. He knew it'd been a slim chance asking to keep this quiet. The scoop was too juicy. This was front page news for their little town and a chance to criticize another Greystone.

Walker started stacking bricks into a pile. His shoulders slumped. The promise to take care of his family and the business seemed to weigh more than the aged pile of bricks scattered around him.

He turned as a door opened. Rebecca, Aunt Bell and Beth stood in the alley staring at the debris of bricks around him. Rebecca had just witnessed one of his biggest failures.

What else could go wrong?

Chapter Ten

Rebecca poured two cups of steaming decaf coffee into the blue floral cups Bell set out after dinner. They'd rescheduled the celebration dinner after the disaster with the crane today. Instead of going out, Bell had whipped up a meal. Grant, Robert and Parks scarfed it down and went to the job site to help Walker.

Bell pulled out the ice cream scooper. "One scoop or two?"

"One." Rebecca set the coffeepot back onto the warmer.

Bell scooped vanilla ice cream on top of the slice of still-warm apple pie that was on each plate. "Grab your pie and coffee, and let's go enjoy the sunset."

They walked out onto the back porch. Bell took the rocking chair while Rebecca settled onto the porch swing.

Vibrant colors spread across the back pasture as the sun began its slow descent. The cows munched on grass, their tails swishing to an unheard tune. She breathed in the scent of earth, pine and summer. The sun sank lower and the orange hues of sunset turned into early evening. She toed the swing as she took a bite of the warm apple pie. "Yum. I see why Walker recommended your apple pie for the baking contest."

Bell chuckled. "He'll do just about anything to get his hands on sweets. All the boys love desserts."

"Really?"

Bell smiled. "Yes, their mother was the same way. She could never pick a favorite. Grant likes peach cobbler, Robert prefers pound cake and Parks loves a good pecan pie. Vince, my sweetie, he loved buttermilk pies."

"I'm sure they are on their best behavior, so you make their favorite dessert for them."

Bell shook her head. "Oh honey, they don't have to bribe me. The boys can bake too."

Rebecca stopped midbite. "Wait, the guys know how to bake?"

"Oh yes. While I love the family God granted me, I didn't cotton for the typical female role."

"Really? We are in the south, right?" Rebecca said, smiling.

Bell grinned back. "We are. I helped Hank with the book-keeping for the business while we raised the family. Working all day, then coming home, and cooking and cleaning for everyone would have been too much." She shrugged. "Besides, I wanted them to be self-sufficient. Hank and I taught them to do their own laundry, make basic meals and how to make their favorite desserts."

"How in the world did you get them to do that?" Unbelievable. She stared at Bell with new respect. She taught teenage boys to cook, clean *and* bake?

"I made it a competition."

Rebecca took note of the twinkle in Bell's eye and the wide smile on her face. "But you didn't make it a regular competition because then they would have guessed." Rebecca toed the swing back into motion. "Wait, don't tell me." She mulled it over. "I get it. You said they couldn't do it."

"Bingo. But making them self-sufficient was my husband's idea. Hank said we all dirtied the house. So we could *all* clean it."

Rebecca slid her now empty plate onto the end table. "Amazing."

"You should have seen the messes they made back in the day." Bell shook her head.

"Aunt Bell, are you telling my secrets?" Walker strode onto the porch, his plate of chicken-fried steak, green beans and mashed potatoes in one hand and a towering glass of sweet tea topped with a dessert plate with a large slice of apple pie in the other.

"I'm not telling your secrets, Walker." Bell shook her head.

He arched an eyebrow. "Right. Aunt Bell, I know you just can't resist. Besides, you know you're not supposed to tell lies."

"I didn't say I wasn't telling secrets. I just said I wasn't telling *your* secrets." After a pause, she grinned. "I'm telling all the Greystone boys' secrets. I was just about to tell her my favorite story about you-all."

"Please, no."

Bell ignored Walker and turned back to Rebecca. "The boys once tried to make biscuits and gravy."

Walker groaned. "Aunt Bell, no."

Bell's laughter tinkled in the night air. "I don't know what the boys were thinking, but they pulled the biscuits from the freezer bag and started tossing them around the kitchen."

Walker swallowed a huge bite of chicken-fried steak as he leaned against the porch railing. "It wasn't me that time, Aunt Bell."

"No?" Her eyebrow rose.

"Nope." He shook his head and pointed to his chest. "I was making the gravy."

"I walked into the kitchen to find frozen biscuits being thrown from boy to boy around the kitchen. Well, some biscuits stuck together. Vince threw a biscuit and it landed in the watery gravy Walker was stirring." Bell spread her arms out wide. "It splashed everywhere, bounced up, knocked over a jug of orange juice before it finally landed on the floor. Walker had gravy in his hair, on his face, and barely any in the pan."

"Oh my, what happened next?" Rebecca's lips twitched as Walker flushed.

Even in his embarrassment, Walker was handsome. He'd come straight from work, his jeans dusty and soiled. He had to be tired and stressed after the damage to the building today. But here he was, listening to his aunt tell embarrassing stories about him. Even with his mouth full of food, Walker stayed put, listening to stories about his childhood antics. His obvious love for his aunt tugged at her heart.

Yes, he was the kind of man she'd always wanted in her life. If only things had turned out different. The last thing Walker would want was to tie himself to his late cousin's pregnant ex-girlfriend.

"Then Hank walked in, and that was the end of the biscuit throwing contest." At Bell's slap of the knee, Rebecca forced herself to refocus her attention on the conversation. "Was Hank upset?" Rebecca loved hearing about their big family. Growing up, it was just her and her mom.

"To the boys he seemed furious, but he really wasn't." Bell waved her hand in dismissal as she wiped away tears of laughter with her crumpled napkin. "He winked at me as the boys scrambled to clean up the mess."

While the story was amusing, it didn't seem gut-busting funny to her. Rebecca looked at Walker.

"Are you waiting for the punch line?"

Rebeca nodded.

Walker's lips twitched. "Aunt Bell snapped a picture of me wearing a pink ruffled apron that said Baking Queen, and that photo ended up on my senior page in the yearbook."

"Ouch, that must have been brutal." Rebecca could hardly imagine how that must have played out at school for a teenage boy.

Still chuckling, Bell rose and gathered up the empty dessert plates. "Good times. Have a seat, Walker. I'm going to go finish up the dishes and turn in."

"I'm fine right here, Aunt Bell."

Bell pointed to the vacated seat. "Take a few minutes to relax."

"Yes, ma'am." Sidestepping the rocking chair Bell vacated, Walker slid into the empty seat beside her on the swing.

Bell stopped in the doorway leading back into the house and said, "Walker, joy always comes in the morning. Remember that—it may seem dark now, but God is faithful."

"Can He make that wall fix itself, because I spent all day trying to find a solution for the repairs."

Bell gave him a smile that could light the whole ranch. "Don't you worry. God will make this turn out better than before. You'll see." Then the screen door closed behind her, and the sounds of running water trickled out to join the quiet of the evening.

Walker let out a sigh as he leaned his head back and closed his eyes.

Rebecca gently toed the swing to move.

He turned to her and opened one eye. "So what do you think? Any guesses at tomorrow's newspaper headlines?"

"Actually, people are already tweeting about it."

Walker slumped down even farther. "Tweets too?"

"With pictures."

"And here I thought the biggest stress of the job would be obtaining the equipment after the mix-up." He rubbed his temples. "Unbelievable."

Rebecca felt the need to alleviate some of his stress. Even though it wasn't her place. Walker had a family to help him. But tonight, out here, defeat affected his whole posture. She couldn't help but want to ease the worry caused from today. They were friends, right? Surely it was natural to want to help him, as a friend.

Walker let the peace of the country evening wash over him, and after a day like today, he sure needed some peace. The familiar cadence of insects trilling was welcome after the fiasco today.

"You're so fortunate to have this." Rebecca waved a hand over the backyard.

He could just make out the beginnings of stars twinkling in the sky as the sun said good-night.

It was good to be home.

"We all are. Our lives could have turned out so differently." Walker stopped the swing.

"Right," Rebecca responded. "I'm so frustrated by where I am in my life. I never thought that after earning a master's degree I would end up jobless and homeless."

Walker sat forward, elbows on his knees. "You aren't jobless or homeless anymore." He nudged her knee with his elbow.

Rebecca made a face. "If it weren't for your help appealing to Beth's and Bell's kind natures, I would be."

"Vince ever tell you how we ended up with his family?"

"He said your parents had died."

He rubbed his hands up and down his jeans. "It was a little more than that, if I'm honest."

"What do you mean?"

From the corner of his eye, he could see she was curious. "My father was an abusive alcoholic. Nobody understood what my mother saw in him or why she stayed with him." He cleared his throat. "They were high school sweethearts."

"I'm so sorry." Rebecca squeezed his arm. Before she could pull away, he reached for her hand and held it. Her skin glowed against his work-roughened hands.

"At my father's insistence, they moved to the next town over to get us away from Uncle Hank and Aunt Bell's reach. Mom enrolled us in school, took a waitressing job and tried to make our apartment a home. She'd earned a full college scholarship but gave it up because she was pregnant with me."

Rebecca's eyes were soft with compassion.

"She turned it down. For me." His shoulders slumped. "And for what?" He'd failed his mother in so many ways.

She nudged him with her shoulder. "Go ahead. I'm listening."

One more thing he admired about Rebecca—her willingness to listen, to be present. She made opening up about the past a little easier. He tightened his grip on her hand, unwilling to let it go.

"When Mom got pregnant with Parks, my father went off the rails because they couldn't afford another kid. He was angry most of the time, even more with another baby on the way. It was touch-and-go for several months, since his job in construction was weather dependent. But honestly, we never knew what would set him off."

He gripped his thigh, squeezed, as if that would stop the avalanche of memories. "They'd argued the night before. He'd shoved Mom into the door frame. When I heard her cry out, I opened the door a crack. I knew better than to let him see me. She was on the floor while he stood over her yelling."

"Oh, Walker."

Rebecca's whisper barely penetrated the memory.

"Even with him yelling, Mom motioned for me to close the door. She always protected us. I should have been able to protect her."

"There was nothing you could have done, Walker. You were just a little boy." The concern in her eyes reached a place he didn't want to feel.

He ran his free hand through his hair. "Whenever he started acting wild, Mom would invent some task or game that kept us in our room. She'd painted our room, added stars on the ceiling. It was a small two-bedroom apartment and dingy by most people's standards, but Mom made it a fun place. I had problems reading, and after being on her feet all day, she'd cook supper and help me with my homework." He rubbed his thumb across her hand. "I don't know how she did it."

"That's what mothers do." She shifted to look at him.

He toed the swing back into motion.

"While she was alive, she was amazing. Worked hard to make sure I didn't miss out on things because my father wasn't around."

She nodded, her smile bittersweet. "I didn't realize that we both had rotten fathers. It's not something I want to have in common with anyone."

Walker nodded. "We had Uncle Hank and Aunt Bell, and you had your mom."

"Yes, we did." She nudged him again. "Quit stalling, continue with the story."

He cleared his throat. "My father stormed out afterward. I crept out once I knew the coast was clear and helped her to bed." He swallowed. "The next morning, she barely made it to the couch."

"And your brothers? Where were they?"

"Enjoying Saturday morning cartoons in the living room while I finished washing the breakfast dishes."

"Even back then, you were responsible."

He shrugged, not knowing how to answer.

"How old were you?"

"Maybe twelve? Mom tried to get up and, when she did, she collapsed on the floor."

Rebecca gasped.

"I've never been so terrified in my life," Walker told her.

"Mom told me to call the ambulance. I ran to the phone. The dispatcher wanted to keep me on the phone, but I passed it to Grant. Mom was breathing heavily on the floor. I held on to Mom's hand. She prayed and prayed. Tears running down her face. And all I could do was sit there and hold her hand."

Rebecca leaned closer and whispered, "You were there for her, Walker. You did the best you could."

He swallowed past the knot lodged in his throat. "Mom asked me to get her book from the secret place."

"Secret place?" Her gaze sought his.

"She kept money and stuff hidden, so my dad wouldn't take it. She hid the important papers and rent money in an old stockpot in the back of the kitchen cabinet. Dad never cooked, so he wouldn't have a reason to find it."

"What was in it?"

"Contact information for Uncle Hank and Aunt Bell."

"She had to keep that hidden?"

"Dad had forbidden contact with her family."

"Why?"

"Uncle Hank tried to get her to leave him. After that, Dad never let her talk to them. He didn't want anyone trying again. And it worked. We didn't see them until that day."

"Oh, Walker." Rebecca moved closer to him. He could smell the sweet lotion she used. She smelled of lemons.

"The last thing she told me?" He pinched the bridge of his nose and blew out a breath. "Take care of my brothers. That's all she asked. And I've tried to do that every day since."

"Even Vince?"

He grimaced. Look at the poor job he did with Vince. Vince, who should be here, with this beautiful woman at his side expecting their son.

"Even Vince. If it weren't for Aunt Bell and Uncle Hank, I don't know what kind of life we would have had. Our father couldn't hold down a job. Everything was always someone else's fault. With Uncle Hank and Aunt Bell, we got a chance to experience a real family. After a few years they formally adopted us." He struggled to continue. He turned toward her. "The reason I'm telling you this is because I want you to know that while you're in a rough place now, it doesn't mean you're stuck there. Back in the day when I prayed my siblings would stay asleep so they wouldn't hear my drunken father, I never imagined my life would be like it is today. God is always with us. He is always there for us."

"Put like that, I guess you're right. I shouldn't complain." She gave him a smile, but it didn't quite reach her eyes.

He slid her hair behind her ear, swept his hand across her lower face in a gentle touch. "I didn't say you didn't have anything to complain about. How Vince left you was wrong."

She stared at her hands. "Maybe he wasn't wrong. Maybe there is something wrong with me."

He ached to pull her close. "There is nothing wrong with you, Rebecca. You are perfect." He wanted to lean in closer to her, but it wasn't his place. He was just a friend. One with an unwelcome connection to her ex.

"How would you know?"

"Because I knew Vince, and I know you."

She shrugged, not believing him.

He lifted her chin and looked into her beautiful eyes. "Rebecca, the reason I told you about my family, is that your past relationship with Vince doesn't have to determine your future. You can make a fresh start. And you have family, right here in Eden, ready to help."

"But I'm not real family." She picked at invisible lint off her dress.

He laughed. "I dare you to tell Aunt Bell you're not real family. Just as Aunt Bell took us in, we've taken you in. You can start fresh here."

"A fresh start, huh?" A small smile tugged at her lips.

At the look of hope tinged with a dash of uncertainty in her eyes, he gave in to all his instincts and pulled her close. The sweet smell of lemons enveloped him. He toed the swing into motion as he felt the pressure from the day ease.

"A fresh start," he whispered.

She laid her head against his shoulder. The moon, bright against the midnight sky, made the darkness of the past fade.

Light instead of darkness.

Joy instead of mourning.

Maybe Aunt Bell was onto something.

Chapter Eleven

Rebecca headed to the cart of books to be reshelved, her mind busy trying to find options to Walker's problem with the bricks. As expected, the damage to the library made the Eden newspaper's front page. The headline Local Contractor Destroys Town's Library was so over the top. She scanned the rest of the article on her phone. As expected, they eviscerated Walker and continued to offer updates on how bad it was. How could she help him? She felt like she had a front-row seat as he tried to fix the problem with the many meetings around the library between JC Construction, the mayor and Walker. Nobody looked happy, especially not Walker.

Shoving her phone in her pocket, she pushed the cart forward. Her first stop was the craft section. It was the one section of the library she would never visit on her own. Crafts were not her thing. She had to jiggle the cart left to right to get it to move because of a bum wheel.

She paused at the adorable baby pictured on the cover of a crochet book. She traced the outline of the baby's face. If Mom were alive, there would be two, if not three, crocheted blankets already in the nursery. A nursery she didn't have. She shook her head and set the book in place. A foster child, Mom had always said her rough childhood had made her a better mother. It was a choice, she'd always said. You could feel sorry for yourself or allow the circumstances of your life to make you stronger.

Rebecca sighed. *I'm trying, Mom, I'm trying.*

"What was that sigh for?"

Rebecca jumped, bumped the cart and it toppled over. She reached to pull it back, forgetting that being pregnant had thrown her balance off. She tried to brace her arm around her baby bump before she hit the metal cart.

Strong arms suddenly grabbed her from behind and enclosed her and the baby in a firm but gentle grip. He caught her seconds before she hit the metal cart.

"Hey there. None of that falling stuff." Walker took two steps back with her in his arms as he pulled her to safety. She gasped and leaned her head back against his strong chest.

Her heart thundered as she gripped the arms holding her.

"You're okay. Breathe."

She sucked in a lung full of air. And another. That was close.

While they stood together in the quiet of the library, he rubbed her arms. "It's okay. You didn't fall. The baby is fine. You're fine."

She opened her eyes. The overturned book cart lay on its side, books scattered on the floor. Could she not do anything right? All she had to do was reshelve books—a simple task.

Tears leaked out of the corners of her eyes.

"Walker, if I can't restock books without an accident, how in the world will I take care of a baby?"

"Come on, none of that." He shifted her so she faced him, leaning her head into his chest.

"It's my fault I startled you." She squeezed his waist and kept her face down, still attempting to catch her breath. She inhaled. He smelled like hard work and sunshine, and his arms around her made her feel safe. No, no, no. Those thoughts were dangerous. Giving herself an internal shake, she tried to focus on what Walker was saying.

"I hate to tell you, but you're kind of front-heavy right now...so."

She almost choked. Did he just say what she thought he said? She glared, not sure if she should laugh or be insulted.

At his attempt at an innocent shrug, she laughed. "Did you just call me front-heavy?"

He stepped back. Hands in the air as if in surrender. "Um..."

"It's called pregnant." Why did she suddenly feel adrift. And why did being in his arms feel so safe?

He nodded. "Yeah, pregnant. That's what I meant."

She rolled her eyes. "Tactful, you are not."

"At this point, I'm not going to answer. I sense I'm digging myself into a deep well." He righted the cart, causing the rest of the books to hit the carpeted floor.

She squatted to gather them up. "What are you doing here anyway?"

"Getting more pictures for the mason so he can repair the wall." He shoved books onto the cart.

She glanced up at his weary tone of voice. He had bags under his eyes. Probably unable to sleep after the accident.

"For the past two weeks, I've been to four different masons—from here to Houston and back trying to find a solution."

She suddenly felt terrible about all her complaining. He had way bigger problems to face. "Walker, I've got this. You need to get those pictures to the mason as soon as possible. Besides, I have to put all the books back in order." She sat down to recategorize the books surrounding her.

Walker bent down and ran a hand through his dark, wavy hair. She couldn't help but notice how his company polo emphasized his muscles as he stretched to help with the fallen books. This close to her she got a good whiff of his cologne, something woodsy that smelled way too good.

"We can get this done quicker together." He continued to stack books, one knee on the floor.

"What quotes have you received so far?"

"Not a one. Matching the color is an issue because the bricks are old. It would be time-consuming and costly to match them. Time, I don't have."

She dropped the book and sucked in a breath. Pressing her hand on her now lopsided pregnant belly, she said, "Whew, this little guy likes to move."

At his curious look, she reached over and put his hand on her side. "Feel." Sure enough, the baby gave another swift shove to her side. She gasped at the pressure.

Walker's mouth opened, but no sound came out as he stared. The baby kicked again, causing both of their hands to move. The air between them suddenly grew heavy, and she forced her eyes to avoid his gaze.

"Does he do that a lot?"

"More and more." She liked the way their hands looked together. Joined in a way she could only wish for. She had to make herself face reality. They were friends. Nothing more.

"Does it hurt?" He moved his calloused hand in a gentle circle. She chanced a quick peek at his face. Her heart tripped, and it wasn't from her near miss. If she was honest with herself, it was from his nearness and the look of wonder on his face. She swallowed. "I expect it will later, but right now, it's just uncomfortable at times."

"Feeling him move, what a miracle. Thank you for allowing—"

"Rebecca, did you fall?" Beth rushed to her side.

Walker jumped up. She was a little empty at losing his touch.

"It's my fault, Beth. I startled her, and she tipped over," Walker admitted.

"What?" Beth glanced from the cart to Rebecca.

"No, it wasn't his fault."

Walker shook his head in disagreement.

Beth stopped them both. "I had problems with that cart last week. I should have thrown it out then. I'm sorry, Rebecca."

Beth turned to Walker. "Would you go get another one, please?"

"Sure thing." Walker walked away, his long-legged stride eating up the distance.

"So, Walker, huh?" Beth wiggled her eyebrows in question.

"He's been very kind to me." Rebecca cleared her throat. More than kind but she shouldn't read too much into that.

"Just kind?" Beth pointed her finger where they'd been sitting. "That looked way more than a 'just kind' moment."

Eager to change the topic, Rebecca said, "I'd better finish sorting these books."

Beth was not deterred. "He's a nice guy. All of the Greystones are, despite what some people in this town might say."

Rebecca picked up a book, flattened a bent page and stacked it on the cart. "We're just friends, Beth." Saying that out loud made her face reality. With her past—and future—that's all they could be.

Beth reached over and tapped her arm. "He's not like Vince. He's responsible and stable."

She stilled. "Those were the qualities I thought I had in Vince. Look how that turned out."

"Walker is an amazing guy if you ever do decide to pursue something with him. He's the real deal."

"The problem isn't me wanting a relationship. It's the Greystones accepting me." She squeezed her eyes shut.

Beth shot her a cheeky grin. "Trust me, based on what I just witnessed? He's interested."

"Yeah, well, I thought Vince was all-in, but he wasn't. And I can't make the same mistake again." She rubbed her belly. "I'm determined to provide a good life for my baby. He comes first." She'd had enough rejection to last her a lifetime.

Beth handed her the last book. Rebecca put it in the right stack, but the cover caught her eye.

"That's it. That's the answer." This was the answer to his problem. Finally, she could help him, pay him back for all the kindess he showed her.

Rebecca showed Beth the cover of the book she held.

"What's the solution?" Walker rolled a new cart over and piled books onto it.

Rebecca turned to the book's table of contents, handed it to him and tapped the page.

"Painting is the answer?" He arched an eyebrow.

She hit the open page again. "Kind of. Look at this." She may be losing her heart over him, but not her mind. Rebecca cleared her throat. "It's the answer to the brick problem. If we paint a mural over it, we won't have to worry about matching the color of the damaged bricks to the rest of the building."

"You want to paint the brick another color? Paint the entire wall?" Walker and Beth glanced at each other.

"No." She pulled the book out of his hand and flipped more pages until she found the description of the front cover picture.

He stepped closer for a look. "You can paint a mural on the wall, something about the town of Eden. Maybe its origins?"

Walker stared at the page. She could see the wheels turning. She continued. "It would hide the problem of matching the brick color, *and* boost the town's history. You wouldn't have to paint the whole building, just the side where the brick doesn't match."

Rocking back on his heels, a dimple appeared in his cheeks as he smiled. "That might actually work."

Beth clapped her hands. "Might? The mayor will love it."

Walker hugged her and dropped a kiss on her cheek. "You're the best! I'm going to talk to the brick company right now." He ran down the stairs, disappearing from view.

Rebecca sucked in a breath, but she couldn't hide the fast-rising blush covering her tan skin.

Beth laughed. "I'd say from that blush, he's a good solution, and from the look on your face you think so too." She moved the cart away as Beth's laughter at her blushing trailed behind her.

Could she try again? Should she? With Vince's cousin? Touching her flushed face, she couldn't help feeling giddy inside at Walker's kiss.

Walker stopped by his truck, parked in the back of the library. He had a pep in his step after visiting the mason after talking to Rebecca this morning. The brickwork could definitely be done in time if it didn't have to be matched to the original brick. He grabbed a Gatorade from the ice chest in the back of his truck. Anything to not think about the fact that he kissed Rebecca. It had just been a friendly peck on the cheek. But why was he obsessing about it so much?

"Hey, Walker, any news?"

He turned around and saw Beth and Rebecca standing outside the library. Rebecca had her lunch kit with her. He set the Gatorade on his toolbox and met them in the middle of the sidewalk. Rebecca wore a maternity T-shirt with the words Read One More Chapter on it, blue jeans and tennis shoes. She wore her long hair pulled back in a ponytail.

"Great news. The mason said if he only has to replace the bricks, not match the color, he can have it done this week."

Beth reached out with a fist bump. "That's great news."

Walker bumped Beth and then Rebecca.

"I'm meeting the new artist in town."

Beth laughed. "Who knew the boy who squeezed a peanut butter and jelly sandwich into a library book would be getting a mural depicting the town's history."

He grimaced. "Okay, now how do you know that was me?"

Beth grinned as she elbowed Rebecca. "It was for sure a Greystone, but none of them ever would admit to it."

"Rebecca, want to walk over with me to talk to the artist? It's a new place a few shops over called The Artsy Place. I could use your help since I don't know what questions to ask."

Beth looked at him, her eyebrows raised and her smile wide. "That's a great idea. I don't know why I didn't think of it myself. You are great at this stuff, Rebecca."

Rebecca fiddled with her handbag strap. "I don't have any experience with murals. I just saw it on the book cover."

He grinned. "Perfect, since I don't have any experience either. We'll help each other. Come on, I'll even throw in lunch."

"That's a great idea, Walker." The librarian glanced from him to Rebecca and smiled. He knew that smile. He widened his eyes to Beth as if to say there was no story here. They were just friends. But from Beth's continued grin, she wasn't buying it.

"I'll check on you-all later. Let me know what happens."

Beth waved, and he guided Rebecca along the sidewalk. They turned toward the town square. The courthouse was built in the center of town, and the four blocks surrounding the courthouse were typical small-town stores. Some of them still had traditional brick decor and awnings, but the Sweet Shop had updated its storefront.

"Have you been to the Sweet Shop yet?"

"No, but clients and the staff have raved about their treats." He walked next to her, aware that they had caught the attention of several people around town. He knew he was in for it. Soon enough, the town would try and pair them together. He opened the glass door to the bakery. The bell tinkled as he walked in. Sandy Lynch, the owner, stood behind the counter. The smell of sugar and yeast greeted him. He spread out his hands to encompass the eating area. "Sandy, I love what you've done to the place."

Twin dimples decorated the peppy blonde's face. "Thanks, Walker." She came around the display case, which was filled with bread, pastries, doughnuts and muffins, to greet them.

"Hey, Sandy, this is Rebecca Young. Rebecca, this is Sandy Lynch. If you need anything sweet or savory, she's the person for the job."

"Nice to meet you, Rebecca," Sandy said.

"Your shop is lovely," Rebecca said.

Sandy glanced around her shop. "We worked hard to balance the old town feel with a touch of modern." She smiled. "How can I help y'all today?"

He nodded toward the open archway leading to the art studio. "I heard a new artist moved into the space next door, and I wanted to commission her for a job."

"Elle Peters? I think she's in. She's probably preparing for today's class." Sandy pointed to the door marked Office behind the second archway.

He headed to the doorway that connected the two businesses and motioned for Rebecca to join him. The decor transitioned from bakery to arts and crafts in ten steps. To the left, artwork hung on a wall, for sale, and to the right were easels and an open-concept classroom. Before he could ring the bell on the glass display case, the office door opened. A woman in her late thirties stepped out. Her hot pink T-shirt read The Artsy Place.

"Hello. I'm Walker Greystone, and this is Rebecca Young. I'm looking for Elle Peters."

She held out her hand and noticed a blue paint smear on it. "Sorry. This is a job hazard." She grabbed a rag from the counter, wiped her hand and stuck it out again. "I'm Elle Peters. How can I help you?"

"I'm trying to find out the logistics of painting a mural on the side of the library building."

Her eyes widened. "The one that was damaged by the crane?"

He winced. "Yes, that one."

"I take it you're the HVAC guy or the guy tasked with fixing it?"

Everyone in a small town knew your mistakes. He held up his hands in surrender. "How about both?"

She laughed. "I used to work for an electrical company way back in the day. Stuff happens on job sites every day. None of them planned."

His brows rose in question. "I sense an interesting story. From electrical company to artist?" He saw a shield slide into place as she shrugged.

"Gotta make a living." She pulled out a notepad. "I just have a couple of questions."

"Shoot." He leaned against the counter.

"What do you want the mural picture to be, and what size? What's the deadline for completion?"

He paused. "Before I can commission you, I have to get approval since it's going on a government building."

She nodded, making notes in the margins as she spoke. "That's no problem. But I need an idea of what you're looking for."

"That's where Rebecca comes in." He turned to Rebecca, who had stopped before a painting of a caterpillar and a butterfly. Somehow, he'd stopped seeing her as the pregnant ex-girlfriend of Vince and started seeing her as something more.

Her excitement showed through her dark eyes as she asked, "How hard would it be to create a mural depicting Eden's history from its founding?" Rebecca asked. "From horses and buggies to automobiles. A mural that would make the town proud. I'm thinking of leaving a space for picture taking since that kind of thing is big on social media."

She continued. "Based on what I've seen on the city's website, the mayor is all about community, and being green. If we include a place to take pictures on the mural, it'll appeal to the community, get noticed on social media and bring more people to Eden."

Rebecca was brilliant. Walker beamed.

Elle tapped the pen on the pad. "That's going to take some thought. I haven't fully researched the town yet."

Rebecca reached into her bag. "I researched some specific dates, and prominent people." She pulled out a notebook, tore out a sheet of paper and placed it on the counter.

Walker once again couldn't help but be impressed. "And you said you wouldn't be able to help."

Rebecca shrugged. "I was noodling around today after you left. The mayor may be a hard sell, so I put on my marketing hat."

Elle laughed as she read the list. "Honey, based on this list, you can put on your marketing hat for my store anytime."

Rebecca blushed as she caught Walker's stare. Something in him was starting to want things he had no claim to. She was beyond his reach.

Elle tapped the list. "With this, I can easily prepare a few mock-ups for you."

"It will be a rush job. We need it finished before the library's grand opening in September."

She cocked her head to the side. "The entire side of the wall or half?"

"The crane hit the top of the building, so the entire side. But the top can be sky and clouds and stuff. Nothing crazy." He internally gulped at what this was going to cost. He wanted it to be an easy job for her. He knew the profits on this job were tanked, but he had to ask.

"Cost?"

She shook her head. "I won't have a number until you decide on a mural design."

He pushed his hat back. "Can you do it? I mean, can you fit it into your schedule?"

She thought for a moment. "I have two projects already on the calendar. I can't make any promises since we don't know the scope of the work, but I will try."

"Regardless, Elle, I'm glad you came to our town."

Elle smiled. A bit of sadness shadowed her eyes. "I may not have liked the circumstances, but I enjoy small-town living."

He looked over at Rebecca, and knew they both thought the same thing. Before he could say anything, Rebecca added, "Fresh starts are good, even if sometimes they start a bit rocky."

Elle closed her book. "That's what I keep telling myself.

This is my new home, so I'll do my best to accommodate you. But the sooner you decide what you want, the sooner I can start."

He handed her his business card. "Can you email me your ideas?"

"I'd be happy to. Give me a couple of days."

He placed his hand on Rebecca's back to escort her out of the store. "So, how about that lunch I promised you?" Just then, his phone buzzed. He read the text. Drat, problem on a job site.

She must have read the look on his face because she said, "It's okay, Walker. I brought my lunch. Besides, I have a lot to do at the library. I know you have a lot going on too. You go ahead." She gave him a small smile and darted off before he could object.

He watched her as she retreated, her ponytail bouncing with each step. Rebecca had saved him with this mural idea, and Walker knew it. He pictured her as the baby moved this morning. Holding her close made him want things he never thought were an option. He wouldn't mind spending forever with someone like Rebecca, who fought for her child's future regardless of the circumstances. Could he ask her to start fresh with him? Or would he forever be in Vince's shadow?

Chapter Twelve

Walker dropped a shovel full of broken bricks into the wheelbarrow. He wiped the sweat running down his face with his sleeve. He'd been loading bricks since early morning, and for the last two hours the sun seemed to shine directly on him. Between the humidity and the beating sun, he couldn't wait to finish. Everything about this job stunk right now. He guzzled down a bottle of lukewarm water as the remaining pile of broken bricks stared back at him.

The side doors to the library pushed open, and Rebecca appeared with a bag of trash. Today, she wore a bright yellow graphic maternity top with a bee on it that said, Bee Kind, Bee Sweet. He couldn't help but grin.

"I didn't know you were out here."

"Figured I would start clearing up this mess." He jerked his chin toward the bricks. In reality, the mason could have done it for an extra charge, but doing it himself saved on the cost.

"I guess it won't clean up itself."

"Yeah, no."

"How did it go when you pitched the mural idea to the mayor?" she asked him.

Walker moved more bricks with the wheel barrow. "He

was leery at first but when I told him I was picking up the tab, he become more enthusiastic."

"Sounds about right. Did Elle get back in touch with you?"

"It's only been a few days, but she sent me an email letting me know she'd have something for me to look at later today." This would end up costing him a fortune, no doubt. Trying to be positive, he determined if all he got out of this was the ability to bid for another job with JC Construction, he would call it a win. He wiped the sweat from his brow and took a breath. His muscles burned from moving the bricks, strain radiating up his spine. He felt the weight of each load he moved. The financial pressure was mounting. One of the company's truck's mileage was over three hundred thousand miles and broke down last week. But he knew that God would see him through. He was faithful. Walker learned that from Uncle Hank and Aunt Bell.

"Yikes, I bet it will cost a pretty penny." Rebecca bit her lip. "I didn't think about that when I suggested the idea."

No way was he going to tell her he would have to put the cost of the mural on a credit card. His financial challenges were the last thing he wanted to share with her. He was supposed to be taking care of her. He shrugged. "It's okay. It's a great solution."

"I've been racking my brain for what else we can do. What good is a mural if no one comes to look at it?" She spread her arms, indicating the space around them. The dingy walls in the alleyway, and the broken bricks all gave off don't-want-to-be-here vibes. But the consequences of not repairing the building were unthinkable. He had to make it right.

At her baffled look, he realized she was still holding the trash bag. "Sorry, I'm just frustrated, and it's not your fault. And here I've got you standing here holding trash. Let me get that. You shouldn't be taking the trash out anyway."

She handed over the trash. "It's not that heavy. Besides, I needed a break from moving books around the library."

"Must be bad if you wanted to come and hang out in the alley with me."

He lifted the lid of the dumpster and dropped the bag inside.

"Why does it smell so bad out here anyway? What could the library be putting in the trash to make it stink like that?"

"The library shares the dumpster with The Artsy Place and the Sweet Shop." He nodded to the building across the alley.

"Oh, that would explain it."

He shoveled more bricks and dropped them into the wheelbarrow. He had another dozen loads to empty before he even made a dent in the stack. When he turned, Rebecca's head was tilted, and she turned around in a circle.

"What are you doing?"

"What else can we use the space for?"

"What do you mean?"

"Do you think we can move the dumpster?"

He shrugged. "I don't know. There is room on the other side of the building, I guess. But why would you want to move it?"

"Just go with me." She shot him a bright smile.

"Okay."

"What if we moved the dumpster, took your pile of bricks and made a raised flower bed? Maybe add a water fountain in the middle of it. Do you think there is room for that?" Her eyes glowed with excitement as she saw possibilities he couldn't. Although he didn't think this was possible, for her he would try.

"Let's see." Walker nodded.

She reached down and grabbed a few bricks from the wheelbarrow.

"What are you doing?"

She grinned, her smile wide and her eyes bright with excitement. "I'm a visual person, so if we use these bricks to section off the areas, I can see it better."

His heart pounded a little as she smiled, and he didn't want to think about what that meant. Instead, he reached down and grabbed a few more bricks. "Lead on." They walked to the end of the alleyway.

"If we put the flower garden here, with a water fountain," she said, pointing to the areas. Then, he set down a few bricks to create a loose semicircle.

She stepped back three feet. " And if we put turf grass in this area." She stooped and set down four bricks to outline her side.

He walked back, picked up more and placed them where he thought she wanted them. She nodded in approval. He liked how well they worked together, bouncing ideas off of each other. It reminded him of the relationship Aunt Bell and Uncle Hank shared. Not something he hoped for himself.

She nudged his shoulder. "If we add a mural, move the dumpster, add the water fountain for aesthetics and add seating areas, it could be a gathering place for people. Maybe parents can bring the kids out of the library if we add green space for the kids to play. It's hard for them to be quiet in the library, and they could use the break between story time sessions."

He stopped. "You know, it could work." She smiled, and her entire face lit up with excitement, sending a rush of sensation straight to his chest. He was excited about this idea, too. That was it. Because there was no way he should be thinking of more with her. She'd volunteered to help tutor some patrons' kids with reading. She'd never told him. One of the moms mentioned it to him last week, and he couldn't help but be amazed by her kindness. The community didn't realize how many grants she'd applied for to fund the new computer room.

"Does the Sweet Shop start at that wall?" Rebecca pointed to the opposite wall in the alley.

He cleared his throat, forcing himself to focus on the conversation and not on how much he liked her when she was close. "Yes."

She shook her head. "Right, and you said we share the dumpster."

Rebecca tapped her foot. "Do you think Sandy would be willing to serve people out here? Maybe put an order window in or something? I remember the ladies in the library saying the Sweet Shop had awesome coffee."

He thought about the previous contracting work he had done for the Sweet Shop. "They do. I did the remodel, and they could easily put in a to-go window. Kind of a drive-through, only a walk-up. I think Sandy would be interested in doing something like that."

"That's great. Then this whole area becomes a gathering place for the community. In fact, I think that's what we should call it. The Gathering Place." She clapped her hands. "It's a win-win for everyone."

"Now, I just have to pitch this idea to the mayor." He shoved his hands in his jeans and leaned against the wall. "That will be fun." His stomach tightened at the thought.

"I know a way you can pitch it to help push him toward saying yes."

"You do?" He quirked an eyebrow. "Tell me."

"With the election coming up next year, he's been busy

talking about the town going green, doing more recycling and stuff, right?"

"It is."

"You can recycle the broken bricks as an exterior for the flower bed. That means you're recycling and utilizing the bricks that are part of this old library. Plus, we can add recycling canisters out here. Wouldn't the mayor love that?"

"Are you kidding? I think he will love every part of this."

But even as he was saying that, he realized how much this was going to cost. He didn't want to think how disappointed she would be if this plan failed. He had to reel in her excitement.

"This is a great idea in concept, but I can't afford to do all of this," Walker admitted. He swept his arms over the imagined space. He took a deep breath before adding, "Not sure how I'm even going to afford the mural." He hated telling her the truth, but it wasn't like she hadn't had a front-row seat to this whole fiasco. How would he come up with the money to pay for everything when he still needed a new service truck? He straightened up and went over to the wheelbarrow.

Walker could handle just about anything life threw his way. But he wasn't sure he could deal with seeing the disappointment in her eyes.

Rebecca could see that Walker was frustrated and weary. She desperately wanted to wipe away the worry in the wrinkle of his brows. Rebecca could see the kind of man Walker was. He pretended he could do anything no matter what— which made his confession about not having enough money dearer to her. It meant that he felt he could confide in her. He was always taking care of others. It made her want take care of him. She bit her lip. She could her heart pound as she realized, she already cared more than she should. But how could she not help? Even in a small town, a project like this would cost thousands of dollars. She wasn't ready to give up, and couldn't give up on him.

Rebecca picked up a couple of bricks and added them to the wheelbarrow. "What about donations? Can we ask the community to contribute?"

Walker laughed bitterly. "This all started because the crane hit the building when I installed the package unit. There is no way we can ask for community donations. Did you see how the local newspaper flayed me alive? Remember the social media posts?"

"Okay, okay." She patted his arm.

"Hmm, we can check out garage sales for the tables and chairs."

"That's a stretch, but what about the mural, the turf grass, the water fountain?" He started pacing back and forth. There had to be a solution. They just had to find it.

"What if we ask the local landscaping business to donate the water fountain in exchange for advertising or something?"

"That's a thought."

Just then, her phone pinged. "Sorry, I have to check this."

"Everything okay?" he asked.

"I have my phone set up to alert me to any emails from Beth. She's asking for a status update on the computer room grant."

He nodded as he kicked the brick debris around.

"I've got it." She could barely contain her excitement to push the words out.

At his questioning look, she said, "The bricks."

"Yes, bricks and high winds got me in this mess."

"No, the bricks, the debris, the restoration."

"I'm not following." He cocked his head in question.

"There's a beautification grant available for the town of Eden."

"A beautification grant?"

She waved her phone in front of them. "Yes. I signed up with this organization, and it sends emails when grants are available. Any grant. There is a beautification grant, and I'm pretty sure fixing up this alley would apply."

"Even if that were the case, do we have time to write the grant, apply for it and get approval before the grand reopening? There's no way."

She squeezed his arm. "Walker, I bet no one has applied, and it's for this budget year. The actual application for the grant isn't hard. It just requires an essay on what we want to do and why, along with the estimated costs."

"You think we can get it?"

She spun around and headed to the library. "Come on, I have half of the essay already written in my head. Can you give me the cost breakdown in half an hour?"

"Are you kidding? This is what I do for a living. I can give you prices for everything except the mural."

"Let's do this." She opened the door, and Walker followed.

Finally, she could offer something to help him, not just ideas. Now, all she had to do was pray they received the grant. "Can you call Elle Peters and get a price?"

Walker stopped. "I can do better than that. I'll head over there and text you the prices for everything."

"Perfect."

When she went back to her office and turned on her computer, she opened her emails to find the grant.

Thank you, God.

Writing the essay was easy; the words just flowed for all the reasons she gave Walker.

She checked her phone. No messages.

Come on, Walker. Send me the prices. She tapped her foot. Something like hope thrummed through her. Because this would help Walker and the whole community. And so far, she had enjoyed being part of Eden.

Finally, her phone beeped. There it was. She typed the categories and the prices into the grant application.

Lord, please let this go through. Not for me but for Walker.

She let out a breath and hit Send. For once, she felt she'd contributed to helping Walker instead of vice versa.

She texted Walker. I just submitted the grant.

Wait, already? he texted.

Yes! Now we pray.

He sent her a thumbs-up emoji.

She texted back, Okay, you can probably use some of that Walker Greystone charm too.

I have charm?

Her face warmed at what she just typed. Dumb, dumb, dumb.

You know you do. The contact person is Diane Knocke. You might try some of that Greystone charm on her. I have no doubt you know who she is.

Her sons and I played basketball in high school.

I knew it.

Off I go! By the way, nice to know you think I have charm.

Her face was burning. She held her phone, frozen. Bubbles popped up. Then stopped, then showed up again.

Then a winky face emoji appeared.

He wasn't flirting. He was just being funny. Right?

But why did her heart flip at the thought of him flirting with her?

Chapter Thirteen

Rebecca put the swing into motion on the back porch. She needed some peace because according to her book, the list of things a newborn baby needed was extensive and she didn't have the funds right now. Rubbing her stomach, she whispered, "I promise, little guy, we'll have a good home. One that's ours." She gazed over the pasture to her right, the neighbor's cows grazed under the Saturday morning sun. In her mind's eye, she envisioned Walker romping through the pasture with two littles by his side. One on his shoulders, and one holding each hand. Who would be the lucky woman walking beside him? She shook her head to dispel the image. It couldn't be her. *Rebecca, focus. Focus on your son.* That's who deserved all her attention right now.

During her visit with the local ob-gyn yesterday, she'd sat beside a husband and wife in the waiting room as they discussed the upcoming birth of their child. She'd felt a stab of envy at the love that radiated between them. What caught her attention most was their discussion about a will and a guardian for their child if something were to happen to them. She couldn't stop worrying as she realized how fragile life was. She'd lost her own mother, from cancer. But Mom had been smart enough to leave a will behind to take care of her money and worldly possessions. It was something she had to do as well. But who would take care of her child?

She turned to the lake as ducks floated by, the ducklings following in their momma's wake. A family. Meanwhile here she sat by herself. Alone again. She hated that. *Get over it. This is life, this is reality.* But she didn't want it to be reality for her son.

Who could she trust to watch over her son if something happened to her?

Aunt Bell? No, that would be too much for her.

Walker? Her pulse leaped at the thought.

As if her thoughts summoned him, a text from Walker popped on her phone. Got a head start on the booths. They are ready for paint.

She smiled and texted back. Way to go, Superman.

Ha, left the cape at home. Too hot in the workshop.

Should she go? It's not like she had anything on her schedule. Walker had agreed to make several booths for the re-opening, and she shouldn't be surprised he followed through.

Providence? He would be someone she could trust with her son. She could ask him today. Setting the dilemma aside, she got up. It was time to paint the booths for opening day.

"Don't worry, little man. We are going to get through this." Her stomach moved. She'd take it as his version of a fist bump from the womb.

Walker propped up the cut plywood against the wall in his workshop. He pushed sawdust out of his way with his work boots. If only he could tamp down his thoughts about Rebecca too. But like the pesky sawdust they floated right back.

He set another sheet of plywood in place. Whenever the

subject of Vince came up, he saw the pain appear in her eyes. He would do anything to make the pain go away.

But if he were to pursue Rebecca romantically, would he forever be in Vince's shadow? Grabbing another piece of wood, he measured again to ensure they were exact; otherwise, the panel would not stand.

Kind of how he was feeling right now. He needed something solid to stand on in this situation. Was he capable of being in a relationship and not mucking it up?

He slid his safety glasses in place and flipped on the saw. How would it affect her life if he pursued a relationship with her and it didn't work out? It could drive her from Eden. She needed support with a baby on the way. And Aunt Bell needed to be close to her grandson. Plus, he didn't know if Rebecca even wanted a relationship with him. Much less with the cousin of the man who abandoned her. He was forever living his life trying to escape other people's shadows.

Turning off the machine, he set the safety shield in place, and grabbed the nail gun to put the booth foundation together. It was definitely better to play it safe than risk driving her away.

"Hi, Walker." He jerked, shooting the nail into the wrong place in the piece of wood.

He pivoted as Rebecca and her very pregnant belly came into the shop. Today, she wore a baby blue T-shirt over white shorts with rhinestone sandals. Her hair was up in a messy bun. Her smile seemed to chase away his dismal thoughts.

"Hi, Rebecca. What brings you here?" His heart beat a little faster, and he knew it had everything to do with the woman who had brought sunshine into his workshop.

"You said the booths were ready for paint." She held up a paintbrush. "I'm here to paint."

He pointed toward the four stands. "Those are ready."

She walked around them. "You are multitalented."

He shrugged. "Being a member of Family Faith Church, you learn to be handy with tools."

"How so?" She tilted her head in question.

"The church throws a Family Fun night, a night just for kids to enjoy games every fall. We build about a hundred game booths for that night and pass out barrels of candy."

"That must be nice." She examined one of the booths.

"Nice?" he asked.

She pushed a piece of curly black hair behind her ear. "To be part of something. To have skills that people count on."

He felt his cheeks grow warm. Come on, he was too old to blush, wasn't he? But he couldn't stop the pleasure her words brought. "Nah, the hard part is the artwork. I can cut anything but drawing and painting? No, thanks."

He pointed to the list pinned to the wall. "I have no idea where Aunt Bell came up with the crazy booth ideas."

She raised her hand. "Guess that would be me."

"You're kidding. Seriously?"

"We wanted the booths to be interactive for the children." Rebecca put her finger over her lips and said, "Not your typical, 'Shhh, you're in the library' quiet event."

He walked to the wall with the list and measurements. "Who came up with Hoop for Books, Fall for the Books, and this one is my favorite, Leap for the Book?"

Rebecca waved her hand, her eyes twinkling with suppressed laughter. "They sound silly, but the kids will love them. Wait until you see them leaping around like frogs."

"I'll take your word for it." Walker took a deep breath. "When I texted you, I didn't think you'd come today."

"I didn't have anything else going on, so I figured why not." She examined the second booth.

He slapped his forehead. "Wait, should you be around paint in your condition?"

"We are using a zero-VOC paint for the booths. Don't worry, the baby will be safe." She returned to the shop entrance, and he noticed a transparency machine on the floor.

"Let me get that." He strode over and picked it up. "Where do you want it?" He stepped back. "I didn't know you were artistic."

"I'm not." She pointed to the machine. "I find a picture, copy it onto a transparency and use the machine to illuminate the image. Then, I draw the outline of the image onto the wood."

She moved to the middle of the workshop. "Do you have a table or something I can set the machine on?" She waved to the area in front of the booth.

"Yeah, give me a minute. I can set up a makeshift table." He set it down and pulled two sawhorses close together. "Where did you learn how to use the transparency machine to draw?"

"Google, then YouTube." Rebecca said.

Walker set a half sheet of plywood on top of the sawhorses to act as tabletop.

"Perfect." Rebecca retrieved her bag from the entrance, pulled out a file of transparencies and set one on the machine. "Do you have an extension cord?"

"Yeah, I have one around here somewhere." He pulled down an extra cord from the wall.

"By the way, I love your man cave," she said as she wandered around the space.

"Man cave? Ha! This is my workshop."

"This is the most organized place I've ever seen. Did you renovate it?"

"It used to be a horse barn. I turned each stall into a storage closet. Albeit more of an open storage closet."

"As I said, very organized." She peeked into each space.

"I have to be. With the construction projects, it's easy to lose a tool. Milwaukees are pricey."

He flipped on the machine. "It's ready. And hey, thanks for giving up your Saturday for this. I'm sure it wasn't on your to-do list for a relaxing Saturday."

Rebecca pulled a bag of markers out of her purse. "I don't have anything going on during the weekends."

"I thought you were going nursery shopping with Aunt Bell."

She shrugged. "Maybe next week."

Rebecca adjusted the size of the image until a frog filled the plywood area. With her profile to him, the baby bump was pronounced. She was beautiful before pregnancy, and now she was even more so.

She turned to him before he could avert his gaze. "What?"

Heat rushed to his face. "I wanted to see if I made the piece big enough."

Feeling stupid at getting caught staring, he pivoted to his work area to clean up the mess. They worked in silence as he put away his tools.

He didn't look her way until he pulled the bag out of the trash bin. He was surprised to see she was almost done with the first outline. "That was quick."

"Tracing is easy. The next part is time-consuming." A quirk of her lips was his only warning. "Want to start painting?"

He laughed. "Definitely not. I'm not artistic."

She tapped her chin with the closed end of the marker. "But you do remodels, which have to involve painting every now and then, right?"

"Mostly I do the AC work. Robert handles the remodel side of the business. Besides, when I help out on those jobs I paint rooms, not frogs and stuff." He motioned to the outlined frog on the booth.

"It's not unlike painting walls. And it's all traced out for you. All you have to do is color in the lines. You learned that way back in kindergarten."

He chewed the inside of his lip as he debated internally. She needed help. It only made sense to help. That's all it was. Helping. Not because he wanted to spend more time with her.

"You talked me into it," he finally said, reaching for the green paint.

As he opened the lid, she asked, "Have you heard from the mayor about the mural? Did they approve it?"

He stirred the paint. "They approved the mural but not exactly what's going to be on it. They're thinking of the birth of the town, its founder and some history, but I'm not sure what. The mayor is happy. He said it's a win-win for everyone."

She clapped. "Way to go, Walker! Making lemons into lemonade or, in this case, turning bricks into murals."

He laughed and winked at her.

"Think the newspaper will pick up the story?" she asked him.

"Are you kidding? The mayor will insist on it. Any chance for publicity." He painted the belly of the frog. "How about the grant? Any word?"

"Not yet, but I expect to hear back soon."

"The wait is frustrating, but I'm glad we were able to apply. But enough about that. Tell me how your week went. Did you have your doctor's appointment?"

She stopped and pushed her hair back behind her hair. "I did."

"Everything okay?" He dipped the paintbrush into the paint. Silence.

He stopped. Something had to be wrong. She stared at the wood, not tracing. Was something wrong with the baby? With her? "You're awfully quiet over there."

She stood next to the plywood, but the marker never touched it.

"You're making me nervous, Rebecca. What happened?"

"They told me everything was fine." She tried to give him a brave smile. "But while I was waiting, I overheard a couple discussing updating their will in case something happened. It made me realize that I don't have anything or anyone in place for my son. My Auntie Grace is elderly and my cousins are all in New York or Trinidad." She rubbed her belly.

All the moisture left his mouth but he forced himself to respond. "I understand."

"I'm sorry. I should be thankful. I have a place to stay, a job and the baby is healthy. But with my mom gone and now being a single mom myself…" She shook her head and trailed off.

His brain buzzed with questions. Should he offer to be the baby's guardian? He was going to be the baby's cousin, right? He wasn't the father she intended. He could be a stand-in once again. Clenching his jaw, he could see the sadness in her demeanor as she turned back to the outline. The workshop fan hummed, droning on like a swarm of buzzing bees. Walker wanted more. He wanted to offer more, he acknowledged to himself, but that was selfish. What mattered was Rebecca's needs and the baby. Not him.

He tapped her shoulder. "Hey, this little guy will be well-loved. Between Aunt Bell and my brothers." He swallowed. "I want you to know I would consider it an honor if I could stand in. I know I'm not his father, but I promise you

I will be an excellent uncle and someone who will love your child unconditionally if something happens to you." His gut wrenched at the thought of anything happening to her.

Her shoulders relaxed, but she kept her face turned away from him. Stepping closer, he noticed that the line she drew was crooked.

He nudged her shoulder again when she didn't reply. "Hey."

She swiped at her eyes. "Ugh. Pregnancy hormones," she said with a huff.

He pulled her close to his side. "I will be here to help." She laid her head on his shoulder.

She wiped her eyes with her hand, and all he could think of was how much he wished he was the father of her baby.

"Thank you, Walker. I try not to worry, but I have to be prepared for his sake."

His heart heavy, he realized he would forever be standing in someone else's shadow. First his father's, and now Vince's. But for Rebecca, he would do it.

For her, he would do anything.

Chapter Fourteen

Rebecca closed the book as the children trailed out of the story time room. The kids greeted their parents at the door, chatting a mile a minute. She noticed Anthony, an inquisitive second-grader, still sitting in his seat.

"Hey Anthony, where's your mama?"

Anthony shrugged his shoulders. "She's out there." He waved to the library.

He sat in the little blue chair, his legs swinging back and forth.

"Okay, do you want me to get her?" She moved toward the doorway, but Anthony snagged her hand in his.

"Can you read me another story, Miss Rebecca?"

Rebecca checked her watch. She still had another thirty minutes before it was her turn at the front desk.

"Pretty please?" He put his hands together in a plea.

"Sure, why don't you pick one from the stack next to my chair?" She pointed to the front of the room and continued to the doorway, where she noticed a woman speaking with the mayor. For some reason, she had a feeling it was Anthony's mother.

"Found one." Anthony held up a book with a gap-toothed smile.

Mayor Stephenson was a frequent visitor to the library.

Every day, he came to check the progress on the renovations, the AC status and the agenda for the grand reopening. You name it, and he was asking about it, and dropping hints that his daughter was still interested in the full-time librarian position. Every. Day.

Anthony patiently waited for the next story.

"Okay, little guy. Let's see what you picked. This is one of my favorite stories. You have great taste." Rebecca loved seeing his reaction to her praise. "You are such a smart little guy. Can you read the story to me?"

Anthony's face fell as he played with the crease in his shorts. He shook his head. "No."

"Hey," she said, looking him in the eye. "Okay, why don't we read it together."

He shrugged.

"You read one page, and I'll read the other. Deal?"

He shook his head.

"Come on, it'll be fun. Besides, we want to know what Drew says about his new bat."

Anthony eyed the book in her hands and slowly nodded.

"Let's see what's so interesting about the boy with the bat."

She heard the clip-clap of heels but kept reading as Anthony was enthralled in the story.

Anthony paused at the *d*, which many little kids stumbled on when learning to read.

"Anthony, how many times do I have to tell you it's a *d* not a *b*! You will be the only high school graduate who can't tell his *b*'s from his *d*'s," the woman from the lobby mocked as she strode toward them. Her voice was shrill and loud in the peaceful room. Her hair was in a tight bun, and she wore a chic gray pantsuit with a crisp white shirt, and a single strand of pearls at her neck.

Anthony froze at this mother's words. Rebecca swallowed the words on the tip of her tongue. With one statement, the woman had undone the past twenty minutes of confidence she'd built.

Putting on her best professional happy face, Rebecca stood and stretched out her hand.

"Hi, I'm Rebecca—" The woman waved her aside before she could give her full name.

"Yes, yes, I know who you are. You're kin to Bell Greystone."

Well, at least she was considered family. "Anthony, why don't you put this book on that cart over there for me?" Rebecca pointed to the cart across the room. She was hoping for a bit of privacy while he returned the book.

"Yes, ma'am." He skirted around his mother, his head bent and steps slow.

"Anthony just has a little trouble reading. I believe it's—"

"He's just lazy. I refuse to let him follow in his father's footsteps." The woman glared.

Rebecca steeled herself against the arctic look the woman tossed her way. Instead, she tried again. "He's very intelligent, and a lot of little kids struggle telling their *b*'s from the *d*'s."

"I told you he's just lazy." The woman stared at her with disgust as she took in Rebecca's maternity dress with a set of handprints from the rambunctious toddler who had run into her earlier.

The woman's voice had become rather loud, and Rebecca could feel the stares from the library patrons through the open double doors. A quick glance proved people were staring, and one was the mayor. Great.

"Nobody asked for your opinion. Come on, Anthony." The

woman tugged Anthony's arm as she dragged him away. His feet barely touched the floor.

Rebecca dropped into the chair. She hadn't even gotten her name. "Great job, Rebecca, way to make a good impression," she muttered to herself.

"That was brave." Rebecca looked up to see Bell enter the room.

"It guts me every time I hear a parent speak to a child like that."

Bell settled into the extra storyteller chair, a rich green armchair wide enough to hold two people. "Me too. That was Rita Stevens. She's had a rough go of it. She's the local attorney, and her husband was caught cheating on her."

"Why did she tear into Anthony like that? I just want to help. He can't control what his father does."

Bell patted her hand. "This is a small town, honey. It's hard when your private life is open for everyone to see. Especially the embarrassing moments."

"Still, Anthony shouldn't have to suffer for his father's mistakes."

"We all suffer one way or another. Just ask my boys. They know that painful truth all too well. Every day they walk out the door, they feel they must prove themselves."

"Prove what?" She shook her head, bewildered.

Bell sighed. Sadness lined her eyes. "As you might already know, Walker's mother was my sister-in-law, Hank's only sister. Bless his heart, Hank tried to get Walker's mother to leave Trevor. He was her high school sweetheart. Well, Trevor turned out to be an alcoholic who beat her. Several times, the police were called. It became the focus of local gossip for a good long while." Bell rubbed her hands down her pink slacks.

"I'm sorry, Bell."

She gave her a watery smile. "We were best friends. In fact, she's the one who introduced me to Hank." She swallowed. "Eventually, Trevor and Walker's mother, Judy, left town with the kids, but not before everyone knew what was going on. When she left, she hoped for a fresh start. Instead, it only got worse. Her husband cut off all communication with us. She never returned—not alive anyway."

Bell pulled a tissue from her white cardigan pocket and blew her nose. "When we got custody of the boys, I was so relieved, yet I felt guilty at the same time."

"Why guilty? You took in her children. I know you were the best thing for them."

Bell stuffed the tissue in her pocket. "I was full of contrasting emotions. Angry because she chose to stay. Bitter because she wouldn't make better choices for the children. Frustrated because I couldn't help her. She was Hank's sister, and he wanted to protect her. Lord knows we tried numerous times to get her to leave. But she wouldn't. I felt guilty because, in the end, I was glad the boys were safe with us. But being with us meant they weren't with their mother."

It was Rebecca's turn to pat Bell's knee in comfort.

Bell sniffled. "Ugh. I didn't mean to get so emotional. Or even bring up Walker's parents."

"It's okay. I understand about being emotional. Especially these days."

Bell chuckled. "The point I was trying to make before I got sidetracked is that the boys feel like they have to prove they aren't like their father or grandfather."

"Their grandfather was an alcoholic too?"

"Yes."

"Oh, I had no idea." That explained so much about Walker's sense of responsibility and his determination to make things right.

"Don't get me wrong. I love our small town of Eden. I wouldn't want to live anywhere else in the state of Texas. But like Rita, when you have someone in your family who does something that draws the wrong kind of attention, you feel like you have to work twice as hard to prove that you're not them."

Rebecca nodded. "I guess I can understand that."

Bell stood. "Walker especially. He blamed himself."

"I don't understand. He was just a child."

"He was the oldest and felt he should have been able to do more. To make matters worse, none of the boys have closure. Their father just disappeared after their mother died." Bell sniffed. "I'm sorry, I got sidetracked. I came to tell you they need you at the front desk."

Rebecca followed Bell out into the main library, her mind on Walker. He found time to help her, help the town and help friends. He was amazing. Every day, she wished she'd met him before she'd met Vince.

Walker dropped onto the covered picnic table seat after placing his lunch order at the food truck two blocks away from the library. He forced his muscles to unclench as people walked around the town seemingly without a care. He had cares—lots of them. The final package unit was delayed—again. By the time it arrived, if it arrived on time, it would be close to meeting the deadline.

"Just the person I wanted to see." Mayor Stephenson clamped a hand on Walker's shoulder. Next to the mayor was John Beckman, the owner of JC Construction. He stifled a groan—just the people he didn't want to see.

"Mayor, John, how can I help you?" Glad for the sunglasses that shaded his eyes from view, he was sure after his frustrating day, he would not be able to hide his real feelings.

"I'm almost glad that crane hit the building. I cannot wait for this mural." The mayor rubbed his hands together and nodded toward the library as if he could see it from there. "I noticed Elle Peters erected the scaffolding to start the mural."

"Yes, sir, indeed. It's going to be great. Thank you for approving it. She needed a week to get supplies together." Walker noticed John was silent and barely acknowledged him with a chin nod when the mayor greeted him.

Walker was glad someone was ecstatic.

John shifted his hands to his hips. "Will the HVAC retrofits be completed on time? I noticed the third unit hasn't been installed."

He adjusted his cap. He knew that question was coming. "Of course. Just a short delay in equipment delivery."

"Good, good. I knew we could trust you to get the job done." The mayor nodded as he smacked him on the back. "I'm going to go check on Elle. See how she's coming along." The mayor and John walked away, the mayor whistling as he left.

When Walker realized his food was ready, he picked it up and dropped it onto the picnic bench. He bent over his burger to give thanks but instead asked, "Lord, I don't pray much, but could You please let our package unit be delivered soon so we can install it on time?"

He had to try. He'd just agreed to be the guardian of the baby for Rebecca. How could he take care of a child, if he couldn't run his business efficiently?

Chapter Fifteen

Rebecca folded the last of her laundry when she heard the familiar rumble of Walker's truck. Even though they lived in the same house, because her room had its own entrance, she didn't see much of him. But she did perk up when she heard him arriving and leaving the house. Curious, she checked the window and saw Walker headed to her door. She opened it before he could knock.

"Hi, Walker." He leaned against the door, his Western shirt as crisp as his jeans.

"Hey there. Bell asked me to drop off chicken noodle soup and homemade bread to Clarice and Wayne Brown, an elderly couple at our church. I thought you might want to join me." Walker shifted. "They have the, um, petting zoo for the kids. You can choose which animals you think the kids would like on opening day."

"Just give me a chance to slip on my shoes and grab my bag."

"I'll make room for you in the truck."

She rushed to the bathroom, grimacing at her reflection. Not planning to leave the house today, she'd thrown her curly hair into a loose ponytail. It was a mess, and Walker saw. Grrr. At least she was wearing one of her better maternity dresses, a cute floral she'd found at a discount store. She fixed her hair, slipped on her shoes and grabbed her purse. A day out sounded perfect right now. But she was more excited about the animals. Not about spending the day with Walker. Nope.

Walker stepped out of the driver's seat and opened the passenger door. He held her hand as she stepped into the cab and into bread heaven. Those were not butterflies flying around in her stomach. An impossibility surely.

"The bread smells fabulous."

"It's just one of the many things Bell makes. She made you a loaf."

"Wow. Tell her thank you. I'll try not to eat it in one sitting." She rubbed her belly. "The baby loves bread."

Walker slid on his sunglasses as he drove the truck onto the road. "Ready to visit the goats?"

"What goats?"

He grinned. "You live in Texas and haven't been around any farms or animals yet?" His dimples were out in full force as he smiled. Lethal those dimples were.

Struggling to appear calm, she shrugged. "Nope. Hello, Houston, remember? City girl here."

"How is that possible?" He shook his head as he drove.

"I mean, I've been around chickens before."

"But not in Texas?"

"No, in Trinidad. I spent a summer with my grandmother on my father's side."

Walker slowed the truck, pulled onto the shoulder, rolled down his window and waved to someone behind them.

A few minutes later, a huge orange-and-black tractor rolled by.

"Wow, a tractor on the main road." The tractor driver waved as he rolled by, his neon green hat with yellow letters that said Farmer John standing out.

"Is that normal?"

Walker laughed, "You are such a city slicker."

"I am, I admit it, but hey, I'm trying to learn how to be a country girl."

"You're fine as you are." It was impossible to ignore the rush of feelings his words evoked.

He cleared his throat. "Tell me about your grandma's place."

She moved a strand of hair behind her hair. "Grandma let her chickens roam free in her backyard. It was interesting navigating to the outhouse when they were roaming around." Rebecca smiled at the memory.

"Wait, an actual outhouse? Surely she had indoor plumbing?" Walker's brow furrowed in disbelief.

She shrugged. "She got it later, but when I was there as a kid it was only the outhouse."

"I guess you aren't such a city slicker after all," Walker murmured as he turned onto a driveway lined with pine trees.

"What was your favorite thing about being there?"

She had to think about that for a moment. "How much did Vince tell you about my family?"

He cocked his head. "Not much."

"Well, my father is from Trinidad. My parents met and married while they were in college in New York." She fiddled with her bag. "They got divorced after I was born. He went back to Trinidad, and my mom and I stayed in New York until she got cancer."

"What about your mother's family?"

"She was raised in foster homes. She didn't have any real family." She shrugged. "My dad's family is it."

"I'm sorry, Rebecca. That's tough."

It was, but she chose not to dwell on it.

"Are you close to your father's family then? I can't tell if you love your Auntie Grace or are scared of her from what I remember during football season."

She laughed. "Ah, you remember our phone conversations during halftime? It's weird to see Auntie get so worked up about football. It's something she picked up after she came to America. It's truly entertaining to see a five foot tall Chinese Trini woman yelling at the refs on tv. Love or scared? A little of both, I guess. I respect her. And her opinion means the world to me."

"I'm glad for you. At least you had her and weren't all alone. Like we had Aunt Bell and Uncle Hank."

Rebecca swallowed. But she had been alone. She forever felt like she was on the outside looking in even with her cousins.

"Did you enjoy that summer?"

"I was supposed to spend it with my father, but I stayed with my grandmother instead."

"That really stinks."

She shrugged. "He would come visit occasionally, but Grandma was great. She started to teach me to make Trini food. Auntie Grace did too, but still despairs of me ever learning to make callaloo."

"Your macaroni pie is amazing. Is that where you learned to cook roti?" The truck rumbled over a cattle guard.

"Yes. Grandma and Auntie Grace are where I got my love of Trinidadian food—especially the tea. Grandma always made tea for me in the morning and at night before bed. Then there was stew chicken, curry chicken, bakes and salt fish, plus the tomato choka and the roti you like." Grandma had taught her a bit more of her father's culture during those hot summer days.

She couldn't help but smile at the memory of her younger self. "Anyway, chickens. Grandma's chickens were scary."

"Chickens are not scary," protested Walker.

"Huh, she had a mean rooster. He would flap his wings and fly at you if you got too close. I was just trying to feed 'em. I will remember that rooster forever. More than once, I feared for my life. I'd run to my grandmother, who would laugh and say, 'Chile, he's not going to hurt you.'

"Today, I promise you won't see mean chickens."

They pulled into the front yard of a typical ranch house. Walker opened the cab door and helped her down, his hand rough and smooth at the same time. She stepped into the bright sun and wobbled a little on the uneven gravel drive-way. Walker tightened his grip and stepped closer. "Are you okay?" He smelled like fresh soap mixed with East Texas pine trees. Somehow, it was comforting.

She was sure he was just being polite. The hand squeeze didn't mean anything. Nor did the kiss at the library. It wasn't really a kiss, more like a "I'm super excited" peck on the cheek. Right?

Get ahold of yourself, Rebecca.

Walker picked up the blue-and-black stockpot full of soup. She reached for the fresh loaf of bread and followed him to the wood porch surrounded by yellow lantanas. An older couple opened the door and stepped out.

"Hi, Clarice. Hi, Wayne. Aunt Bell heard you were feeling poorly, so she whipped up a batch of her famous chicken noodle soup for you."

"That's right sweet of Bell. Good to see you, Walker."

"Clarice, Wayne, this is Rebecca. She's in charge of the events for the reopening of the library. We thought we'd look at the animals while we are here."

"We've met before," said Wayne. "Don't you worry. I'll be there for the book club."

Clarice coughed into her handkerchief. "What he means is he can't wait to debate with old Stephens."

Rebecca handed over the loaf of bread. "I can't wait. I hope you feel better soon."

"I moved the animals into the barn," Wayne said, motioning to the bright red-and-white barn behind them.

"Thanks, Wayne. We'll go check them out."

Rebecca could feel Walker's gaze on her. "What?"

"Proud of you, meeting people and branching out." His mouth tilted up.

She shrugged her shoulders. "Beth handed over the book club to me. They had a rousing and rather loud discussion over the merits of roses last week."

Walker raised his eyebrows as he led them onto a gravel path behind the house, where the bushes created a hedge along the walkway. "You put Wayne and Stephens in the same room to debate roses?" He whistled. "Brave woman."

"Believe me, if I'd known, I wouldn't have brought it up. I mentioned how pretty the roses were outside, and before I knew it, they were arguing over which type of rose was the best. Not talking about the book they read." She raised her hands in question. "Who knew?"

He grinned. "Those two are opposites on anything gardening. Hard to believe they're cousins."

"They are related? You're kidding, right?" Rebecca stopped as Walker pushed open the red barn door.

"Nope." He ushered her into the dim interior. The smell of hay, earth and farm animals greeted them.

"Could have fooled me," she muttered.

"Don't let them. They play cards every Friday night, have since I've been around." He flipped on the barn light, illuminating a square interior with stalls lined on each side.

"Goodness." She wandered from stall to stall.

"The goats are out back." Walker reached the back of the barn and threw open the back door. "As promised."

"They are adorable." She bent closer to the cross-fenced area housing the goats. "Oh, look, a baby."

She stuck her hand through the fencing, but it pranced away.

"It's called a kid." Walker hitched his boot on the first rung of the fence. "Want to feed them?"

"Could I?" A dozen goats nibbled on the grass across the yard. Two stood on either side of an old seesaw.

"Sure." Walker walked over to the nearest food bin, grabbed a cup of food, opened the gate and ushered her in.

He handed her a cup of the feed. "Shake the cup. It'll make them come to you."

Rebecca bent down and poured a handful of feed in one hand while shaking the cup with the other. The baby goat came right up to her.

"Hold your hand out flat so she can get the food without nipping your fingers," Walker instructed as the kid nosed around her hand. He bent down next to her.

He reached out and petted the black-and-white goat as it nibbled the food. Across the pen, two goats went up and down on the wood seesaw while two more came toward her.

"Oh, they heard there was food." She started to stand.

"Hey, hey." Walker stood up and caught her as she tipped.

She was such a klutz. He seemed to be rescuing her from one catastrophe or another.

"Let's go visit the rabbits. They aren't so fearsome." He motioned to the rabbit area.

They went into the pen, which was scattered with hay. A dozen rabbits were eating, napping, or hopping around in it. Walker opened the pen and motioned for her to follow. He scooped up a white rabbit and handed it to her.

"So, today was the first time I heard you speak about your dad, outside of our conversation on the swings. Do you miss him?" He reached down and picked up another rabbit. There was something about a big man like Walker holding a defenseless rabbit. Strong but gentle, a winning combination. Qualities she wished for her future husband and the father of her son. But she'd have to be both for her child.

She knelt, put the white rabbit down and walked toward another, which was hopping along the pen's edge by itself. "In rare moments." She picked it up, this one white and smaller than the others.

"I'm sorry," Walker offered.

"It's all right." She swallowed back the ache caused by that period of life.

"I even have a half sister. Weird, huh?" She kept petting the little bunny.

"Why is that weird?" He set down the rabbit he held.

"I met her that summer. She was from my father's first marriage. When he and my mom split and he went back to Trinidad, he remarried his first wife." She moved the hay at her feet until she created a bare spot.

"Have you tried to reach out?" Walker leaned against the pen.

She closed her eyes, barely keeping a normal tone of voice. "To my sister? She didn't want to have anything to do with me." She met his gaze, but then looked away, embarrassed by what she revealed. "Hey, you promised me chickens, didn't you?"

"I did, and since I'm a man of my word, let's go." They closed the pen gate and headed back into the Texas sunshine. The smell of hay and the animals faded, but the memories of her father's and sister's rejection remained. Them, plus what

Vince had done to her... How could she even think about trusting someone else again?

They walked back to Walker's truck. "I didn't mean to bring up bad memories."

She shrugged. "That's life, I guess." She rubbed her baby bump. She was determined her son would have everything she didn't have.

He gave her a side hug. She leaned her head against his shoulder as they walked. It felt good for someone to be interested in her life. It was something she didn't realize she missed until recently.

"And here comes the promised chickens."

She picked her head up, alert. "Remember, you promised no mean chickens."

"Oh, I remember." He gave her that dangerous smile. The one with those dimples.

"I'll feed them for you, just in case there is a wild one in the bunch." He stepped away from her to the food bin. Walker grabbed a cup of feed from the covered barrel and ambled closer to the chickens.

"How come the feed is so close to their pen? Can't they get to it?" She stayed back, her feet planted in the grass five feet from the roaming chickens.

"It isn't normal, but Clarice knew we were coming. She wants you to see how easygoing these animals are and why they are good to take to the opening. It's something the kids enjoy, feeding animals." He motioned to the entire farm area. "They love goats and chickens. But I think the rabbits will steal the show."

"But won't bringing just one of each be better?"

Walker shook his head. "No, goats are herd animals and do better together. Plus, having several of each for the kids to pet makes sense. I think you're going to have a big crowd."

"Goats are herd animals. Who knew?" she asked.

Walker motioned to the surrounding area. "Wayne and Clarice have about a hundred acres out here. See that dog over there?" He pointed to the back porch where a mixed mutt lay down. He raised his head to look at them and then lay back down, his tail moving in a lazy wave.

"He's obviously not a guard dog." Walker spread feed around his boots as several brown and tan hens began pecking around him. "Not for people anyway." He chuckled. "She's a protector for the goats. Believe it or not, she's grown up with them."

Rebecca peered through the bright sunshine at the dog.

"Seriously?" The protector hadn't budged since they'd been wandering around the area.

"Last spring, when the goats were dropping kids, she circled around them to keep people away until they were up and about." He drew a circular motion with his arm.

She could sure use a protector like that. Someone to champion her child and put him first. It was something she'd never experienced. She shook off the emotions that threatened to ruin her time with Walker. Deciding that the chickens were tame enough, she reached into the bin and took some feed, spreading it in a circle mimicking Walker.

"I love it out here." She took in the bright sun, the thick foliage at the fence line and the fresh-cut green grass around the barn and farmhouse. She inhaled the sweet country air—everything about Eden spoke of peace and home.

"We may make a farm girl out of you yet."

Rebecca lifted her brow. "Maybe a small-town girl. But a farm girl? That's a stretch." She stepped back as a hen picked at the feed at her feet. Why had she spread the food so close?

"Your Aunt Grace, you haven't told her about the baby yet?"

She shook her head.

"Why not?"

Her stomach clenched at the thought of that conversation.

"Do you have any idea of the expectations of a first-generation American, for an immigrant? Especially a child of mixed parentage?"

He adjusted his hat. "No, but I'm sure she would want to know no matter what. Regardless of expectations."

She blew out a breath. How to explain the pressure to him? "To Auntie Grace, success is a college degree. A steady job. Marriage. Then children. Except I don't have all those things. I have a baby on the way. One that's isn't supposed to come outside of marriage. And that degree? I've got a bachelor's and a master's, but I haven't been able to land a full-time job yet." She turned away to hide the rush of emotions washing over her.

Walker jumped down off the railing and stood next to her. She didn't turn her head.

"You are a success. Sure, it didn't work out with Vince, but you have your degrees and a job."

"A part-time one," she muttered.

"Have a little faith. I know it'll become a full-time position." It was great that he believed in her, but the mayor was still lobbying for his daughter to get the job.

"I know you're right, but how in the world do I tell Auntie Grace? She's going to be so disappointed in me."

"You tell her you fell in love, and even though it didn't work out, you have a baby on the way. And you can't wait for her to meet him."

"It's easy for you to say." She swallowed, her throat suddenly parched at the thought of that conversation ever taking place.

He gave her a side hug. "Maybe. But hey, if you stick

around here, all of us Greystones would love to help him learn to play baseball and basketball and build things. We'll be here to help you through the good and bad times. Owww!"

Walker jumped as a rooster pecked at his foot and another pecked on the other one. He jumped again, and the goat next to him took offense and butted him, throwing him off his feet. Walker landed with a thud on his rump.

Rebecca started to laugh as she wiped the tears from her eyes at his stunned expression.

"Wait—where did that goat come from?" he asked from the ground.

She reached down with her hand outstretched to help him up. "I guess this means I get to help you through the bad times." He took her hand and stood up, pulling her into the circle of his arms. Standing so close, she could smell his cologne. Her pulse raced as he leaned down and waited, as if asking her permission for something. He slid his calloused hand along her jaw. She placed her hand above his. Still, he waited. She reached up on her toes to touch her lips to his. A kiss. A kiss that tasted of hope she never expected to have.

He pulled away from her, let out a breath and leaned his forehead against hers, his voice thick. "I should thank that mean ole rooster." This didn't make any sense, her and Walker. She knew she should walk away. But just for a moment, she got a glimpse of what her tomorrow could look like. And she wanted to hold it close just a little longer.

Chapter Sixteen

~❧~

Walker wiped his hands down his jeans as he stood outside Rebecca's door. He shifted the food from one hand to another. He didn't know what possessed him to kiss her, but he didn't regret it.

Finally, he could admit to himself he wanted a life with Rebecca, if only he could quiet the part of him that believed he wasn't capable. She had been quiet on the ride home after their kiss. They'd talked about inconsequential things. Neither one of them had brought up the kiss, and he was content to leave it that way. At least he didn't get an outright rejection from her. Her gentle smile afterward was positive, right? All week as he worked on the library, she'd given him those smiles. Smiles that actually reached her eyes.

She opened the door in a denim maternity romper. "Walker. Hey."

He held up the bag he picked up after work. The sweet smell of chicken stir-fry and lo mein wafted between them. "I couldn't help but hear you today while you were talking to Beth."

She tilted her head to the side. "Hear what?"

He whipped out chopsticks and brandished them. "I believe you said something about craving Chinese food?"

She opened the door wider. "Chinese food! You're amazing! That's perfect. Come in, come in."

Walker couldn't help but stare. When she smiled, it made him feel something extraordinary. Like maybe he could conquer the world with her by his side.

She stepped back and blew the hair out of her face. She held out her hand to stop him. "Don't laugh at the mess in here though."

"Of course not. What mess?" Walker stopped as soon as he stepped over the threshold. Parts and pieces littered the floor. Pieces of a crib lay scattered around. A wrinkled piece of paper that looked like instructions lay on the floor in front of the couch.

Rebecca closed the door and stood beside him. "Yeah. The crib arrived today, and I thought I would assemble it."

"I see." He was careful to keep his facial expression neutral. Screws and bolts littered the floor.

She threw him a rueful smile. "The instructions seemed simple enough."

"Mmm-hmm."

"You'd think I would be farther along after an hour, but I think maybe they forgot some of the parts." She shrugged her shoulders. "Because I can't figure it out."

He set the takeout on the kitchen counter and followed her into the room where she snatched up the instruction manual. Just then her stomach emitted a low growl.

She put her hand over her growing belly and shot Walker an embarrassed smile. "I guess you brought dinner at the perfect time."

Walker grinned. "You are too cute. Feed that baby while I look at this."

Walker sank down on the floor and studied the instructions. Ah, he saw the problem. He rummaged around the screws and bolts, put them in order by size. He didn't see the next screw size. "You definitely have a set of screws missing."

He swept his hands under the couch just in case. "Yep, here they are." He picked up the Allen wrench and went to work.

She sighed out loud. "Whew, glad it wasn't me. I mean, I know I'm not the best at putting together stuff, but I thought the crib would be easy."

He made short work of completing the assembly. "What do you think?" He stood it up.

"I think I'm really glad you stopped by." Rebecca placed a container of lo mein next to him with a fork, napkin and some sweet tea.

"Once again Walker Greystone otherwise known as Superman swoops in and saves the day."

"Definitely not Superman." He picked up the plate and took a bite. "Man, Bertie Mooks, the chef at the Chinese restaurant knows how to make a mean lo mein."

Rebecca played with the noodles on her plate. She glanced at him and then back at her food. "Can I ask you something?"

He took a gulp of tea. "Sure."

"Why did you kiss me?"

He set his plate down on the side table. "I don't really know." He studied her face. He didn't know how she did it, but she made him want more than just to settle for the life he was living now. Or to accept the voice in his head that told him he shouldn't expect to be happy. He blew out a breath. He had to try. Didn't he?

"You don't know? What does that mean?"

"I… I didn't plan on kissing you." He swallowed. "I like you, Rebecca. A lot. But I don't know if I should be asking for anything more."

Her gaze was steady on her plate as she remained silent.

Could that have come out any worse? He cleared his throat and kept going. "I never thought marriage was in the cards for me, given how my parents' and grandparents' marriages turned out."

She just looked at him as if she waiting for clarification. The problem was he didn't know how ready he was to risk his feelings. Guess he should of thought of that before he kissed her.

"And?" she prompted.

"And you make me want more." At her silence he hurriedly added, "I know that may be an issue because of Vince—I don't want to pursue you if—" He cleared his throat. This was hard. But what had he expected? That she would just let the kiss go and not ask questions?

Rebecca twisted the napkin in her hands. "I… I would like to see where this goes, if you can see past the fact that I'm pregnant with another man's child."

His heart thudded hard as he reached for her hand. "All I see is a beautiful woman who is doing her best to provide for her child. Using every tool in her toolbox to build a life for herself."

After pausing for a moment, she motioned toward the completed crib. "Let's hope that my toolbox for creating a home for this little guy is better than my crib building skills."

He laughed. But on the inside his heart thudded as he realized what a risk he was taking. If this didn't work out, it would affect everyone, especially Aunt Bell and the baby. He knew from experience that a broken relationship didn't just hurt the person but made you question your own worthiness of love. He didn't want that for himself or Rebecca.

Rebecca could hardly believe this conversation. Walker took their plates and washed them in the kitchen sink. She sat back on the couch. She'd gone over the kiss again and again in her head. Convinced herself it was just a fluke. That he didn't really mean to. That it was a one-off.

He thought she was worthy. He wanted to be in a relationship. With her. He made her feel seen and heard. He remembered her favorite herbal tea and delivered on the promised mocha almond fudge ice cream. That meant something, right? That he cared enough to pay attention. And he kept his promises.

She tried to contain the tidal wave of feelings washing over her as she realized he really wanted a relationship *with* her. Thoughts of Vince and his betrayal rose up, but she pushed them away. Maybe the past could just stay in the past. Dare she hope?

Just then her phone rang. It was the contact for the beautification grant. She snatched up the phone and showed him the name on the caller id. He turned off the water and walked toward her. "Hello?"

"Hello, is this Rebecca Young?"

"Yes, this is Rebecca."

"Hi, Rebecca, this is Diane Knocke. I know this is unusual to call after work hours. But I thought you would want to know that you were approved for the beautification grant."

She mouthed to Walker, *We got it!* Walker jumped up and pumped his fist in the air. "Yes!"

Taking a deep breath to act semiprofessional, she said, "That's great news, Diane. Thank you so much for taking the time to call me, even if it is after work hours."

Diane laughed. "That's the beauty of being in a small community. But I have to say, you did an amazing job in the application process. All the information was included, and it was well written. You gave a compelling argument. We all know how much this grant means to the Eden library and the patrons. It will be a great place to encourage community."

Walker leaned closer to the phone. "Thanks, Diane! We will begin construction on this right away!"

"Walker! You're welcome. Rebecca's grant writing skills, and the speed of which she put everything together definitely got your name at the top of the list."

He grinned. "Yes, ma'am. I realize just how special she is."

Rebecca couldn't stop the jump in her heart rate at his smile and wink.

"Thanks again, Diane." Rebecca ended the call.

Walker squeezed her hand and kissed her cheek. "You, Rebecca, are a wonder. You are the one who should don the superhero cape. First the idea for the mural, and now financing to turn the alleyway into the Gathering Place."

She flushed at his praise. But all the details to get it together still loomed. She thought of all the specifics that had to work in concert to meet the reopening deadline.

"How soon can we get started? We only have a few weeks to get everything done. I mean, you know the contractors who are going to transform the alley personally. Do you think they can fit the project into our schedule?"

Walker whipped out his phone and sent three texts. "There is only one way to find out."

She couldn't help but admire him. He had a goal and would keep going until he accomplished it.

He flashed her a smile. "I've texted the landscaping guy about the water fountain and turf grass. I texted Rocky about the outdoor tables and seating. And lastly, I texted Sandy Lynch, the Sweet Shop owner, about putting in a walk-up window. Now, do you have any of that amazing ice cream around?"

She laughed as she rose to get it. Maybe everything would work out with the grand reopening and maybe even her and Walker. She crossed her fingers. If it did, it would be the first time in her life she'd be in a relationship with a person who wanted to stick around.

Rebecca dreamed of their happily ever after last night. Walker would be the kind of husband that helped around the house, like his Uncle Hank. They'd be able to laugh over the crazy things their three kids did. But mostly, he would love her. She whispered a quick prayer to God that her love would find a home.

Chapter Seventeen

It had been a full month since Walker put together her crib. A month of picnics, dinners and working together to put the finishing touches on the grand reopening of the library. Today was the first day of speakers leading to the grand reopening and the festival on Friday. Rebecca exhaled a long breath. She gripped the clipboard and triple-checked her to-do list. Everything was going to be perfect today.

Pulling the keys from her pocket and unlocking the library's door, she flipped on the lights. Lisa Tagg was the storyteller today. It would be incredible to have the author for the Princess Isabell series. Rebecca had arranged the room with an assistant yesterday, leaving nothing to chance.

The speaker would be seated in an old-timey armchair with a wood side table and standing lamp. It gave the room a homier look, as if someone's grandmother was about to read a story. Twenty-four plastic chairs were arranged in a semicircle in multiple rows.

Rebecca straightened the author copies and slid a bottle of water onto the end table. Thanks to the fundraising efforts of the Friends of the Library Group, each child attending today would get a free copy of *To the Library We Go*.

"Knock, knock."

Rebecca turned to see a young woman in her midthirties with wavy brown hair and a winsome smile.

"Hi! I'm Lisa Tagg." She pointed to the lobby. "The lady at the front desk told me to look for Rebecca."

"I'm Rebecca Young." She stuck out her hand. "Thank you so much for agreeing to read to the children today, Ms. Tagg."

"Please call me Lisa. Anything I can do to help the library I grew up in." She pointed outside the room. "I see you've updated the place."

"Yes, this week's events are a celebration of our grand reopening. But if you ask me, the staff is celebrating the completion of the renovations."

"I get it. I started a remodel in my basement and wow, the dust. I can only imagine what it was like in the library."

Rebecca rolled her eyes. "You understand then. I've never dusted so many books in my life."

"I see congratulations are in order." Lisa pointed to her baby bump.

"Thank you. I'm excited but nervous too. He's my first." Rebecca straightened her shirt down. "Do you have any children?"

"No. Mr. Right is taking his time. At least that's what my mother says." Lisa shook her head, her smile wide.

Smiling, she asked, "Is there anything else I can provide to make the reading easier?"

"This setup is perfect." She tapped the stack of books. "Are these the books you want me to autograph?"

Rebecca nodded. "If you could. I know the kids will be thrilled."

"Of course." Lisa slid into the seat, pulled a purple Sharpie out of her bag and began signing.

Before she could make conversation, Bell strode into the room. A soft pink dress had replaced her traditional khaki slacks for the occasion. "The children are starting to trickle in. Are you ready?"

"I am. Lisa, I'm sure you know Bell. Bell will introduce you, and I will be in the back of the room in case you need anything."

"No flying airplanes this time?" asked Lisa.

Rebecca slapped her hand to her forehead. "You heard about that?"

Bell tsked. "Lisa, you shouldn't tease her." The older woman turned to Rebecca. "The little boy is related to her."

Lisa laughed out loud. "Oh, if I could have been a fly on the wall that day. I cannot wait to add that to the next story."

She was sure that everything was going to go smoothly. Even the local newspaper reporter, Jason Black would stop by today to interview Lisa.

"I'm going to open the area for everyone." Lisa and Bell nodded as she made her way to the back of the room and removed the barrier. Outside, a dozen children and parents chatted in line.

"Welcome everyone, welcome. Please take a seat. Just ten more minutes before we start." Rebecca set the yellow barrier under the staircase.

"Miss Rebecca, Miss Rebecca! Look what Mom bought me," Anthony yelled from the line. He was skipping while his mother tried to coax him into a walk. He held a plastic doll of the Royal Prince from Lisa's series.

"It's the prince. Mama says I'm her prince, but she's silly." Anthony rocked up and down in his sneakers. He held up the royally dressed prince for her inspection.

His mother tousled his hair. "You *are* my prince, silly. Go pick a spot for us to sit."

While Anthony scampered off, his mother turned to her. Rebecca braced herself for another caustic comment. But instead, his mother cleared her throat. "I want to apologize. I thought about what you said. I'm sure you know what's happening in my family—Anthony, my everything right now. I want you to know I've been spending time reading with him and you were right, he's already improved." She fiddled with her purse strap.

"It's okay. I understand."

"Momma, come on." Anthony waved her over.

"I better go. Thanks again."

Rebecca *was* making a difference, even if it was in one person's life. She stepped into the room, the excitement of the kids evident in their wiggling bodies and rapid chatter. Within moments the room was full.

Bell introduced Lisa to a rousing round of applause and shouts of hooray from the kids.

Rebecca turned as a volunteer tapped her shoulder. "They need you up front. Mrs. Robin said there's another author here who says she's scheduled to read today." Rebecca signaled to Bell she was leaving and turned to the volunteer. "Please stay and help Bell watch over the kids." The volunteer took her place inside the doorway. She racked her brain. How could she have double booked two authors? Her heart in her throat, she rushed to the front.

Suddenly, her feet slid out from under her. Her eyes blurred as she stared up at the fluorescent lights.

Pain. Sharp pain. She grabbed her side. What in the world? She grabbed her belly as she felt a wetness beneath her. No, please don't let her water break. It was too early. Pain snaked its way up her back and around her stomach.

Someone was asking her something, but she couldn't focus. She forced a breath out through clenched teeth. Suddenly, Bell was there. She grabbed her hand. She tried to sit up but couldn't.

"The kids, don't let them see," Rebecca grunted.

Bell turned to the volunteer. "Go back to room and close the door." The volunteer nodded and disappeared.

Bell patted her hand, "Can you tell me what hurts?"

Rebecca breathed in slowly. She shook her head. Bell leaned in to listen.

"The baby."

Then Bell was talking, but she couldn't see to whom.

"Dale, this is Bell at the Eden library. Rebecca fell... Send an ambulance... It's too early..."

Rebecca opened her eyes and shut them as black spots danced in her vision.

She leaned her head back on the floor. "It's supposed to go smoothly today. They won't hire me now." She whimpered.

Bell gripped her hand. "Shh. Don't you worry. Let's take care of you and the baby."

She lay still and tried to breathe.

Please God, keep my baby safe.

She couldn't lose another person in her life.

Walker entered the library through the back entrance for the last time. All the HVAC systems were up and running, he'd hand in his keys to Beth today. The quiet whir of the new air conditioner was music to his ears. They'd made the deadline. Just barely. His heart had been light for the past month with Rebecca. Just maybe, he had a chance, a chance for a lifetime of happiness. The faint click of typing from the computer room echoed through the first floor as he headed to the story time room. Today was a big deal for Rebecca, and he wanted to support her.

He stopped at the sight of Rebecca on the floor. He ran and dropped down beside her.

"What happened? Is she in labor?" Her eyes were squeezed shut and tears tracked down the side of her face.

Bell shook her head, her worry evident. Rebecca turned to him and reached out. He grabbed her hand and held it. He leaned in.

"It hurts, Walker."

"It's going to be okay, honey." He kissed her hand, looking to Bell for answers.

"I don't know what happened. She hasn't been able to tell me." Bell jerked her head to the room to the right of them. The door closed. "The aide at the back of the story time room rushed out of the room—I happened to be keeping an eye on a couple of girls when she ran out. I followed and found Rebecca on the floor." She patted Rebecca's hand, but her eyes were on Walker. "I called Dale. She dispatched an ambulance."

He nodded. She'd fallen a few steps before the offices, so they weren't visible to the main area of the library.

He squeezed her hand, the sound of an ambulance siren drawing nearer.

He leaned over to try and comfort her. Her caramel complexion was pale. He brushed her hair away from her face. "Hey, I'm right here."

"I'm scared." The fear in her eyes gutted him. He couldn't promise her everything was going to be all right. This scene reminded too much of his mother. He steadied his breathing, for her. He had to be steady.-

He wiped the tears from the corners of her eyes. "Don't worry. The ambulance is on its way." His instinct was to hold her close, protect her. The last time he'd seen a pregnant woman on the floor, it hadn't gone well. He bowed his head and prayed. *God, please.*

The ambulance finally pulled up in front of the library, the squeak of the gurney wheels loud in the quiet library.

Bell rose to make room for the paramedic.

"What happened?" he asked.

"We don't know. Her water must have broken."

"How far along is she?" the paramedic asked as he checked her vitals.

Bell gripped Walker's shoulder and answered. "She's not due till the end of the month."

The second paramedic dropped down next to Walker. Bell tugged her nephew back as the paramedic tried to edge him out of the way. "Walker, please let them help her."

His chest tightened, like it was caught in a vise.

With the sound of the siren, the patrons from around the library gathered. Walker reached for the retractable crowd control barrier tucked under the stairway. As he walked over, he stepped into a puddle. He looked around to find the source of the water. Seeing nothing, he looked up and momentarily froze.

Then he put the barrier in place on autopilot. The paramedics bundled Rebecca onto the gurney. Bell motioned for him to follow, but he couldn't. He stood in the puddle of water, his grip on the barrier crushing.

The paramedic pushed Rebecca into the ambulance and closed the door. Still, he stood there, unable to move. Acid churned in his stomach.

It was his fault that she fell.

He stood in the puddle of water caused by the air conditioner.

Chapter Eighteen

After a night of nurses going in and out of her hospital room, Rebecca was ready for her own bed. She glanced out the window at the overcast sky.

With all the hoopla yesterday, and the relief of knowing her water didn't break, she wanted to rest. Nothing could top hearing her son's heartbeat and seeing him on the ultrasound. To believe that maybe, just maybe, everything would be all right.

She fidgeted with the hospital blanket. While Bell had been with her most of the night, Walker had cried off because of some emergency at work, Bell said.

She opened her last message to Walker. Hey, just wanted you to know we are going home today. Doctors said everything is fine.

She swallowed past the lump in her throat. She couldn't get over the fact he hadn't come by the hospital last night or even texted her. Everything she knew was relayed through Bell.

Did that mean he wasn't interested anymore? Maybe— like Vince—he realized that she just wasn't worth his time? Her fingers hovered over the text as a ragged breath escaped. Everybody left. What was it about her that no one seemed to stay in her life?

Oof. She struggled as the baby kicked.

"Buddy, karate classes aren't for another seven years." The terrain of her pregnant belly shifted. Just like the landscape of her life. She froze, stunned as she realized not everything was terrible. Okay, so the hospital stay wasn't great. And she was sure the subsequent bill would be huge.

She moved again, trying to find a comfortable position. The clock on the wall ticked loud in the silence of the room. She exhaled. Okay, she had to be logical about this. She couldn't afford to be emotional, pregnant or not. She rubbed her belly. She had a little one to take care of. A child who depended on her. She remembered the scripture Pastor Jeff used in his message, Romans 8:28. "And we know that in all things God works for the good of those who love him, who have been called according to his purpose." His reminder that even in the bad things God works them out for our good. God brings something good from something bad. That meant her too, right?

She leaned her head back. When she was in her greatest need, God always sent someone to help. He sent her college friend Carrie David to tell her about the job opening. He'd sent her the Greystone family for a place to live. And He'd provided a part-time job, even if she wasn't sure it was going to turn into full-time. God hadn't left her like Vince or her father. There was something to what her friend Julie had told her the week before she left Houston. God was a good father. Her earthly father may have messed up, but God never did.

She touched the sheets as she forced herself to think objectively. While she may not have her mother or her father here, Bell was with her. She'd accepted her unconditionally and never talked about Vince or why they'd broken up. Bell had shown her how to love unselfishly, and so had Walker.

A smile curved her lips, and for the first time in a long

time, she was at peace. "It's going to be okay, little one. God never leaves us, even when we can't see Him. We are never alone."

Rebecca would never forget last night, waiting for the ultrasound technician to arrive.

Bell had laid her hand on the baby bump and prayed. "Father, the Bible says You knit this little one together in his mother's womb. We ask for good health and a full-term pregnancy as he rests in Rebecca's womb. We thank You for cradling both of them in Your hands, keeping them safe today."

No matter what the future held for her and Walker, God would still take care of her and her baby. She pressed delete and cleared her phone screen.

She wouldn't text Walker.

She leaned back just as the door opened. Walker! She smiled as her heart beat a little faster.

"Hello, Rebecca."

She froze. Auntie Grace? How in the world did she get here? She pushed the button to raise the bed into an upright position. She ran her hands through her hair and tried to straighten her gown. Who was she kidding? There was no straightening a hospital gown when she was round as a beach ball. "Auntie."

Aunt Grace, barely five feet tall, with salt-and-pepper hair pulled back in a bun, rounded the hospital bed with outstretched arms. She enveloped her in a hug full of Trini spices, and, strangely, a feeling of home. Something she deeply needed as she faced a sea of uncertainty with her relationship with Walker.

Auntie framed her face with her wrinkled hands. Hands that bore the testimony of a long life.

"Bell called," Auntie Grace said. "She found my number in your phone."

Busted by her own preparedness. Her sense of responsibility had motivated her to make Aunt Grace her emergency contact.

"Why didn't you tell me you were pregnant?" Though her auntie barely topped five feet, she spoke with the authority and the power of a military general.

She opened her mouth, but no words came out. What could she say to even begin to explain?

"Rebecca, why have you kept this a secret?"

Unable to meet her aunt's eyes, she plucked at the white hospital sheet. "What could I say? 'Auntie Grace, I'm pregnant and I can't even find a job?'" She let out a sob because she couldn't change the facts. Except for the past few weeks, life had been good. Especially between her and Walker. Her situation was getting better. It was only under the ugly glare of old expectations that she fell apart.

"You should have told me exactly that," Auntie Grace said.

"Momma would be so disappointed in me."

"She would *not* be disappointed in you. She loved you with everything she had. As do I." Auntie gripped Rebecca's hand. "We are family. Family means sticking together through unexpected pregnancy and unemployment." Grace gently placed her hand against her baby bump. "But this baby is not a mistake. And your mother? Yes, she would have wanted you to be married so you could have a life partner. But if you don't, well, it's his loss."

Rebecca blinked. Mom would be happy for her. She knew that, so why had she allowed herself to live under this cloud of shame? "Auntie—"

Aunt Grace shushed her. "What I don't understand is why you're with Vince's family? This Bell woman that called me, she is Vince's mother?"

Rebecca nodded. "Yes, they put in a good word for me to

get the part-time librarian position. Walker has been amazing, helping plan the library reopening."

"Walker?" She raised a silver threaded eyebrow. "Who is this Walker?"

"Walker Greystone is Vince's cousin. His mother died, so he grew up with Vince like brothers."

"Why would you put yourself in a position that requires assistance from this family? Or the baby?" She wagged her forefinger. "Are you—" Grace sputtered. "He's related to Vince!"

Rebecca grabbed her hand and squeezed, determined to make her understand. "Auntie, the Greystones aren't like that. *He's* not like that."

Grace held up her hand in the universal demand for silence. "If this Walker is so trustworthy, where is he now?"

Rebecca bit her lip. That was the big question, wasn't it? Where was Walker? She understood if something had come up with work yesterday. But where was he now?

Walker's boots echoed in the sterile hospital hallway. He paused to get a grip on the floral arrangement he'd picked up from the gift shop. He stopped in front of her room, let out a deep breath. He'd battled with himself long and hard. Would she ever forgive him for causing her to fall?

He pushed the door open a crack but stopped at the unfamiliar strident voice inside.

"This Walker, why do you trust him? Look at you in this hospital bed! Where is he? And he's related to that Vince. Come, as soon as the doctor releases you, we will head to New York. Cousin Jay can get you a job at a library. He has plenty of contacts."

He dropped his head against the door. Whoever was in

the room with Rebecca was speaking the truth. Rebecca was in that hospital bed because of him.

Just when he got a glimpse of a future, he managed to hurt the one woman he'd hoped to cherish.

He edged the door open a little farther. He could see Rebecca, garbed in a blue-and-white hospital gown. There were tubes hooked up to one arm as she turned her head to speak to an older lady at her bedside.

He could still picture his mother on the floor all those years ago. Pregnant, pale, scared. He could do nothing then. And there right in front of him, a stranger spoke the truth. He wasn't good enough for Rebecca or her baby.

He'd hoped to tell her what happened and ask her forgiveness. Instead, he turned around and let the door shut on his hopes and dreams.

The truth was crystal clear; he wasn't meant for a family, at least not one with Rebecca.

Chapter Nineteen

Walker had to get out of there now. He'd return the flowers to the florist downstairs and have them deliver it. He held his breath as he punched the elevator button.

He'd spent the night with his brother tracing the water leak. They'd found the problem. One of their employees had connected the PVC but didn't glue it together, which was what had caused the leak.

He should have checked the work. He scrubbed his hand down his face. The elevator dinged, and he stepped to the side when people exited the elevator. The doors slid open and out stepped Aunt Bell.

"Walker. Oh, I'm so glad I caught you! Wait—you still have the flowers? Did they take her for more testing? She was fine when I left her earlier. What happened?" Bell turned to rush toward the room, latching on to his forearm.

He dug in his feet to slow her down. "No, she's got company." At Bell's questioning look he said, "You know, since she has company, why don't you give her these for me. I can give her a call later." He tried to thrust the flowers into Bell's hands, but she refused to take them. Her eyes seeing clear through to his soul. She saw too much.

He flipped his wrist to glance at this watch, thinking maybe she'd take the hint and let him off the hook. Instead, she pulled him in the opposite direction, toward the waiting area and sat.

"What exactly is going on here, young man?"

"Nothing. I went to visit her, and I could hear her aunt talking so I decided to wait till later to visit."

"Her aunt from New York?"

"Wait, you knew she was coming?"

"Of course, I'm the one who called her. What happened?"

"Nothing." He shrugged. "I went to Rebecca's room and heard voices, so I left."

Her right eyebrow tilted up in question.

"I don't know why you're making such a big deal of this. Like I said, she had company, and I didn't want to interrupt them." He shifted the flowers from one hand to the other.

Bell cocked her head to the left. "Walker?"

He sighed, knowing there was no escape.

"I know that she hasn't seen her aunt since she's been here so. I, um, thought it would be better to let them visit."

"Walker. This is me you're talking to. The woman that raised you. I know when you are deflecting, and you are deflecting now."

He shifted his feet again. "I may have overheard their conversation. I may have heard some not so complimentary things about myself."

Bell raised her eyebrow. "From Rebecca? About you?"

He shook his head. "No. Her aunt."

"So, you just left?"

He set the flowers on the magazine table. "What do you want me to do?"

"Stay. Talk to her, maybe explain, but whatever you do, don't leave her like everybody else."

"That's not fair."

"No, you're letting fear rule your actions. Rebecca thinks

you're awesome. And I've seen you two together. You're good for one another. Besides, you had no control over Rebecca falling. You're beating yourself over something that wasn't under your control."

He shoved his hand through his hair. "Oh, I had control over this. All I had to do was check things, and I'd have discovered my employee didn't glue the PVC in place."

Walker jammed his hands in his pockets and paced. "My negligence caused her to fall."

"Your negligence? It was an honest mistake."

He turned to Bell and pointed to Rebecca's room. "Rebecca is paying for my mistake. I'm supposed to be helping her, not making her fall a month before the baby is due."

He took a deep breath and hoped the feeling abated. His best bet was to leave Rebecca alone, before he caused her any more pain.

Bell tapped the chair next to her. "Walker, sit down."

"Aunt Bell, there is nothing you can say that will make this better."

"Sit down right now, young man. This has gone on long enough." When Bell used that tone, a serious talking-to was in the making. He sat immediately.

"What is this about?" she asked.

"Her aunt was asking how Rebecca could trust another man in our family. The crazy thing, Aunt Bell, is that I'm wondering the same thing."

"Why are you questioning yourself?"

"My father couldn't be trusted."

Bell reached over and grabbed his hands.

"Walker, you have a maturity beyond your age, except in this matter. In this, you are blinder than old Mr. Tom with his trifocals."

"But—"

"Shush and listen to me. How can you believe those lies? Most men your age would have gone off to college, partied and maybe a decade later, started to settle down. Instead, you're here, in Eden, Texas, running the family business with your brothers, taking care of your cousin's pregnant ex-girlfriend."

"I just—"

"Just what? The last time I checked, Vince is the one who left that young lady high and dry. Not you." She waved her hands to the room in general. "And then there's this need to prove you're not like your father. Congratulations! You succeeded over a decade ago. Don't you think it's time to let it go?"

"Aunt Bell, you don't understand."

"Don't you 'Aunt Bell' me. Forget the lies people try to throw on you. You are not your father's son. You are your own person. God didn't make you in your father's image, but in His."

She grasped both sides of his face. "I know deep down you still feel like that little boy who caused everything bad to happen. But you didn't."

"But when Mom—"

"Stop. You were a child, Walker. A little boy. Yet you were the one who called the ambulance. You're the one who packed her bag. You. You were the one who kept your brothers until I got there. You. Hear me well. None of what happened to your mother was your fault. Now as far as what you've heard from Rebecca's aunt—it doesn't matter. But Rebecca does, and right now she needs you. Don't leave her like everyone else has." Bell jabbed her finger in his chest. "That would be on you!"

"But—"

"In this situation, right now? It's up to you. Not your

grandfather, not your father. You. Remember what I said. You weren't made in your grandfather's image or your father's—you are made in God's image." She took a breath, then said, "Now, I'm going to go see her and reassure her all will be well. You stay here and think hard. If you let this young lady go, mark my words, you will always regret it." With that, Aunt Bell walked away.

So where did he go from here?

He stared at the ceiling as if it would yield answers. What would she say when she found out he caused her to fall?

He gripped the window frame as he stared over the town. Deep inside Bell's words resonated. He *was* made in God's image, not his father's or grandfather's. From here he could see a glimpse of the mural. The artist was painting an entirely new picture—and he needed to erase the image of himself that he'd been living under. As it said in the Bible, He could do all things through Christ who strengthened him.

Chapter Twenty

Walker squared his shoulders and pushed the door to Rebecca's room open. Relieved when he realized only Rebecca was in the room.

She was sitting upright in her hospital bed. Because of him. Yet, her eyes lit up as he walked in.

"Walker, I'm so glad you came. I was worried about you." She beckoned him closer.

He released his tight grip on the flowers and set them on her stand. "These are for you."

"Thank you. They're beautiful."

He swallowed, not knowing how to start. He shoved his hands in his jeans.

"What is it?" she asked.

Could he do this?

Rebecca reached for him, and he grabbed her hand as if it were his lifeline.

He lowered the bed railing and sat on the edge of the bed never letting go of her hand.

"Walker. You're making me nervous."

"Rebecca— I found this—"

Walker turned as an elderly woman entered the room. This must be her Aunt Grace.

"Who is this?" Aunt Grace demanded.

"Auntie, this is my friend Walker Greystone. I've told you about him, remember?"

Aunt Grace jerked her chin in acknowledgment, her features frosty. "Did you find out why she fell yesterday?"

Walker jumped to his feet, still holding Rebecca's hand.

"Young man, my great-niece was hurt on your watch. Can you tell me if you've found out anything?"

Walker turned back to Rebecca and rubbed his thumb over their connected hands.

"Rebecca, I want you to know I'm sorry you fell. If I could change it a hundred times, I would."

"It's okay, Walker, it wasn't your fault. I was just being a klutz. Probably just tripped over my own feet."

He braced himself for her scorn. "No, that's just it. Your fall was my fault."

"No, Walker, somebody probably spilled water, and I was unlucky enough to find it. You can't take responsibility for something someone else did."

"I *do* have to take responsibility." He shifted his weight, forcing himself to keep eye contact. "You didn't fall in a puddle of water that a patron spilled. It was the new air conditioner." He turned to Rebecca's aunt. "Ms. Grace, I want you to know, I accept full responsibility."

He let out a breath and continued. "I know your aunt has a job lined up for you in New York. But if you give me a chance, I can prove to you why you should stay in Eden. You have a family that cares for you here and will help you with this baby. We won't ever leave you. We believe family takes care of family." Tears welled up in her eyes. It tore at him, but he had to finish. "I know you were hurt by what Vince did. And even though I'm his cousin, I hope I've proven to you I'm nothing like him. Please, stay in Eden, Rebecca. Give me a chance."

The silence was loud in the room, but he refused to look at Grace. Instead, he focused on Rebecca and the tears that rolled down her cheeks.

She didn't say anything. She was going to leave him. A shudder ran down his spine as he realized he lost her. He was tempted to run out of the room, instead he wiped her tears away with his thumb and brushed his hand along her jaw. "I'm sorry. This is the last thing you should be dealing with. Just call me if you need anything."

He kissed her hand and laid it on the blanket. But she held tight. He swallowed, hope rising.

"See, Auntie. I told you he was trustworthy." Trust. Her words sunk into his soul like rain in a desert.

"Walker, I know you aren't Vince. I've always known you're different. I have no plans of going to New York. This baby needs to be around all his uncles, his cousin and his grandmother. You've shown me that family does indeed take care of family."

She pulled him into a hug, and he held him tight. Relief flowed through him as hope filled the empty spaces inside.

He had a chance at a future he never thought possible.

Chapter Twenty-One

Walker checked his watch for the fifth time. Forty-five more minutes and he'd take the biggest risk in his life. The smell of hot apple cider wafted across the street that was crowded with people. Today's turnout had increased as the day progressed. He squeezed Rebecca's hand. She turned, her eyebrows raised. Aunt Grace and Aunt Bell were discussing baking at the pie stand. He shuddered as Grace caught his eye, her scowl evident even after he apologized.

"Why are you fidgeting?" asked Rebecca.

"Because Aunt Grace just gave me the death glare."

Rebecca laughed, as she turned and waved at her auntie. "She did not give you the death glare."

He snorted. "Yeah, she did."

Rebecca shrugged. "Okay maybe. It'll take awhile, but you will win her over. She's protective. She will eventually succumb to the Greystone charm."

"Uh-huh."

She punched him in the arm. "You think *she's* tough? Wait till all my cousins come to town next week."

Walker grimaced. "I can't wait."

Rebecca squeezed his arm as she stifled a laugh. "Seriously, it will be fine. Just give her some time. She's already warming up to you. She loves the mocha almond fudge ice cream you brought over." She jerked her chin in the aunt's direction. "Look, Aunt Bell has won her over."

He looked over, and they were both in a deep discussion, with Rebecca's aunt gesturing with her hands and Bell nodding. They did look like they were getting along. He pulled on the collar of his shirt and checked his watch.

"Walker, that can't be the only thing bothering you. What's really wrong?"

He aimed for a nonchalant grin. There was no way he wanted to give even a hint of what was coming. "I don't know, maybe because my girlfriend is heavy with child and insists on walking around as if she isn't toting a ten-pound baby in her belly."

Her eyes lit up as she laughed. He hoped he could provide her a lifetime of carefree laughter. He shut the door on all the what-ifs and why-nots that jetted through his mind.

"Are you excited about the unveiling of the mural? I know I am. I don't understand what all the hush-hush is about. It's just the history of the town, right?" Rebecca asked.

If she only knew just why the event had been so cloaked in secrecy. He'd called Elle and begged her to add a scene to the mural. Bless her heart, she'd worked around the clock to make it happen. The mayor was across from them, with the newspaper photographer taking photos. Another photo op.

When he'd asked the mayor about his speech, and the additional scene, the mayor clapped his hands in anticipation. Typical politician; the better the headlines, the better the photo op, the better for his reelection. But he couldn't tell Rebecca that. Instead, he answered. "More nervous than excited."

She tilted her head. "Why nervous?"

He didn't want to give anything away, but he had to respond somehow. "We, uh, made some last-minute changes that I hope go over well." He would be forever grateful to God if this endeavor went over without a hitch. And for once, he wasn't fighting the reputations of his father or grandfather when he stood in front of the community. This was for him and him alone.

"The artist added a scene of the town's founding father." She squeezed his arm. "Which one?"

He winked and grinned because he knew her game. "Nice try." A blush stole up her neck but she met his look head-on. "What?"

"I'm not going to ruin the surprise."

She huffed out a breath. "I'm not going to tell anyone."

He chuckled. "It's the principle of the thing. Besides—" he tilted his arm to check the time "—you have thirty more minutes to wait."

People were already using the Gathering Place, strolling in and out. The town created a sitting area for the community to read, watch their kids and enjoy the food next to the bakery. It could have been the scene of his lowest point. Instead, Rebecca had helped him create something to celebrate. He rubbed his hand down his jeans. The beautification grant had come through just in time for the local contractors to get everything Rebecca imagined in place for the celebration. The flower bed, the water fountain, the seating area, and he had squeezed in the time to help install the walk-up window for the Sweet Shop.

"Hey." Rebecca tugged on his arm. "I think you are worrying for nothing. You've given speeches before. Besides, curiosity has been rampant about what's included in the mural. People will be more focused on the mural than you."

"Gee, thanks."

"You know what I mean. While I'm sure people will be interested in what you have to say, there has been a lot of curiosity about what's on the mural. It's been so hush-hush the whole town has turned out for it."

He cleared his throat. "Yeah, that's what I'm afraid of."

"What do you mean?"

He squeezed her shoulders. "Don't listen to me. Even though I've given speeches before this one makes me a little nervous."

She straightened his collar. "Just add a little of that Greystone charm, and the crowd will be eating out of your hand."

He offered up a quick prayer that it would be so.

The microphone let out a piercing screech. All attention turned to Beth as she waved to the crowd. "Hi, everyone, Thanks for joining us at our grand reopening. It's time to unveil the newest piece of art in our humble little town. Let's all head to the alley, our new Gathering Place, where we will unveil the mural. I'm sure you've all seen the new seating area between the bakery and the library. Please join us."

"Ready?" Walker winged his arm for her to hold. She held on to his supporting arm.

"Just the people I wanted to see." They both turned as Beth approached them.

With a glint in her eyes, Beth leaned toward Walker. "Ready to give your speech?"

"Ready as I will ever be."

"Hey guys? What did I miss?" asked Rebecca.

Walker squeezed her hand. "Nothing. Beth's just mad because I got picked to give the speech." He tucked her hair behind her ear. "You promise to stay right here? I'll need your support."

"Of course. Where would I waddle off to?"

He dropped a quick kiss on her forehead and melted into the crowd before turning up next to the podium.

Uh-oh, John from JC Construction stopped him. She wished she could hear what they were saying. Suddenly Walker broke out in a wide grin as John clapped him on the back. That was a good sign, right? She prayed that was a sign that more commercial jobs were in Walker's future. He had worked hard to deliver his very best.

Beth whispered, "Guess what I heard today?"

Rebecca kept her eye on Walker. He was joined by his brothers on the podium. It was rare to see all the Greystone brothers together outside of Sunday lunch. All tall, lean and rugged, they were the epitome of the American cowboy with, cowboy hats, starched shirts, and blazers. All the way down to the starched jeans and scuffed boots.

"I don't know. What did you hear?"

"You are no fun." Beth huffed. "Fine, I'll tell you. We raised $2,000 from the fundraiser."

"That's amazing! It couldn't have happened without you."

"It wasn't me, honey. You were the one that organized everything, made all the contacts and then left detailed lists for someone to follow. Well done. But that's not my good news."

"Um, we sold all the books at the book sale?"

Beth grinned. "Nope, okay fine. You won't guess so I'll tell you."

Rebecca tilted her head. "Okay, tell me."

"We have a new full-time librarian on staff."

What? Someone else got the job? She licked her lips and forced out, "Who would that be?"

Beth's eyes widened in innocence behind her wire-framed glasses.

"Word is she's great at her job, but alas, we were told she couldn't start for eight weeks."

Rebecca gripped Beth's hand, her heart doing double time as Beth's words sunk in. *Eight weeks.*

"You're hiring me full time?" she squeaked just as Aunt Bell and Auntie Grace joined them.

Beth beamed. "Yes, silly. There wasn't any doubt after all the excitement that's followed you around. I mean, come on, you pulled off the reopening without a hitch. It's not every day we get funding for new computers, not to mention the bonus of the beautification grant! So do you accept the position?" Beth waggled her eyebrows up and down.

"Are you crazy? Of course!"

She wanted to tell Walker, but he was onstage. She didn't know how he'd slipped into her heart and filled it up. She had a home and a job. She patted her baby bump as he shifted again, making her stomach look like a ski slope pitched to one side. "God's been good to us."

She pulled both aunties in for a hug. "They hired me!"

"We never had a doubt," said Aunt Bell.

Rebecca wiped the corners of her eyes. "Stupid hormones."

Bell squeezed her shoulder. "You're pregnant dear. Hormones are part of the package."

Rebecca tried to catch Walker's eye onstage. He looked nervous. She wanted to give him a thumbs-up. Mayor Stephenson tapped the mike to gather everyone's attention. The loud thump caused the crowd to quiet down.

"Thank you all for joining us for the grand reopening of the Eden town library. I'm proud to announce that after almost nine months of remodeling, the library has reopened with twenty-four new computers on the way."

The mayor pointed to the men onstage. "I want to thank JC Construction and Greystone Contractors for their outstanding work on this project. Walker Greystone took charge as he normally does, and recommended a mural to depict the history of our town. Now, for what you've all been waiting for. May I present to you…"

The mayor nodded and the person on top of the roof released the curtain.

A round of applause burst from the group as the artist's rendering was revealed. Beautifully drawn, it depicted the humble beginnings of dirt roads, horse-drawn carriages and simple wood-front buildings. Rebecca scanned the wall as she attempted to take in the details. There was an original picture of the Texas Café, the railroad depot and—a proposal scene? What in the world was a proposal scene doing on the mural?

The mayor continued as the crowed quieted. "We hope you appreciate our history as much as the generations of people born and raised here. At the far end, we've added the proposal of Harold Bennington. It's reported that when he decided to stay and make Eden a town, he brought other families with him. He found a wife from among the early travelers. He proposed and named our town Eden because he found his own slice of paradise here with his soon-to-be bride, Rachel Jordan."

"Oh, how romantic, how did I miss that piece of history?" she asked.

Bell held her handkerchief, tears in her eyes. Maybe her pregnancy hormones had rubbed off on Bell.

"With that, I'd like to turn over the microphone to Walker Greystone."

She couldn't keep the smile of pride off her face. He'd done it. He had finished the work by the deadline and received the recognition he deserved.

Beth tugged her hand. "Follow me."

Rebecca trailed after her until they were at the front of the mural.

Walker cleared his throat. "My brothers and I wanted to thank the residents of Eden for trusting us with this project. At times it was challenging, but I was very thankful for the help of Beth Porter and our new librarian, Rebecca Young.

"If you-all will bear with me for a moment." Walker removed the mike from the podium and jogged down the steps. Where was he going?

He headed toward them. Assuming he was going to thank Beth properly, she stepped to the side.

Instead, he stopped in front of Rebecca. She felt her face turn hot. All eyes were on them. What was he doing?

Walked reached for her hand.

"Rebecca Young, I've never been so thankful for a new resident of Eden, as you. You've taught me how to persevere under difficult circumstances. You've taught me to keep going, and most importantly you've encouraged me to be myself. And I hope—" he took a deep breath, sweat glistened across his forehead "—I hope you will want to be part of my future. I promise in front of everyone here today—to love you with everything within me, to be here when you need me and to love your child as my own. To be someone you can trust your whole heart with."

Her eyes widened as he dropped to one knee and pulled out a blue velvet box. When he opened it, a diamond twinkled in the light. "Will you marry me?"

Blinded by her tears she barely get out a "yes." She didn't hear the thundering applause; all she saw was the man she loved, a man who had shown her by word and deed what it was to be loved wholeheartedly. He stood up, brushed his lips against hers and whispered, "I love you."

Epilogue

"Mama, carrots, horses, peaz," Little Henry cried as he ran up the porch steps and latched on to Rebecca's leg. Named after Walker's Uncle Hank, Henry's embrace filled her with joy as she set the bowl of potato salad on the picnic table. She placed one hand on Henry's curly hair to keep him in place as she grabbed a pile of napkins before the wind blew them away. The family had decided to take advantage of the cool September afternoon for their Sunday lunch. They didn't plan on the stiff breeze or the fact that Henry and Bentley were enamored with the new horses on the ranch. Which meant they wanted to feed the horses five times a day. Grant, dressed in starched blue jeans and a green polo, followed the boys up the porch stairs. He grinned as he swung two-year-old Henry onto his shoulders. Bentley brushed by him and squeezed her other jean-clad leg. "Please, Aunt Becca, can we feed the horses?"

Bell and Auntie Grace joined them outside, each setting a pie on the already full table.

"Wow, that's a lot of dessert." Rebecca eyed the huge pies.

Bell laughed. "Have you ever seen dessert go to waste in the two years you've been here?"

"You're right. It's always just enough," Rebecca teased.

"Peaz, Mama," begged Henry again.

"What do you need, sweetie?" Auntie Grace asked Henry, who knew his auntie Grace would say yes to anything he asked.

"Feed horses, Auntie Grace. Peaz." He clasped his hands together.

"Robert and Parks are in the barn. I can take the boys with me. We'll keep an eye on them until lunch is ready," Grant said as he held on to Henry's legs to keep him in place on his shoulders. He pilfered a roll before Bell could stop him.

"Let's all go. Come on, Bentley. We can feed the horses." Auntie Grace beckoned them as she and Aunt Bell headed to the barn. Bentley latched on to Auntie Grace's hand and started yapping a mile a minute.

Rebecca leaned against the porch column as they walked toward the barn. Thankful for the view of the pond adjacent to the pasture where she could see everyone and miles of green pine trees. When Henry was a newborn, she and Walker spent many a night on this back porch swinging him to sleep.

The screen door bounced closed as Walker set the barbecue ribs and chicken platter on the table. "Lunch is ready."

"Those boys have both aunties and your brothers wrapped around their fingers."

Walker strode up behind her and pulled her into a hug. "And you're surprised by this?"

"The aunties? No, but your brothers. A little."

"I'm not."

"Why aren't you surprised?"

She could feel his shoulders shrug behind her. "Aunt Bell thought it was her job to bring in every hurting kid around. We've always had tons of kids at our place. Summertime was always a big party around here."

"I guess that makes sense." She nodded toward the boys.

"Grant thought they would be able to distract the boys, but I bet they will be at the fence line with carrots in five minutes, tops."

"It was a great idea to turn one of the barns back into a horse barn. I'm glad Grant is interested in horses again. At least we don't have to walk two miles to go to the barn to feed the horses or let them out to the pasture." Walker laid his chin on top of her head. "Especially since they ask to feed the neighbors horses every chance they get."

"Uh-huh." She had her doubts about Grant's sudden interest.

"What does that mean?" Walker asked.

"Just that it might have something to do with the new neighbor."

"What new neighbor?"

"The neighbor that's leasing all this acreage from your aunt?"

"Mr. Wilkerson has leased the property since Uncle Hank died and we couldn't keep up. He's not new."

"Yep, that neighbor. He's got a visitor then. One of the young and very pretty variety. She may be the reason Grant is interested in horses again."

"No way."

Rebecca rolled her eyes. Sometimes Walker was so clueless. If Grant didn't want Walker to know he was interested in the neighbor, she wasn't going to say a word.

"Rebecca?"

"And there they are." She pointed to the pasture. Sure enough, the group emerged from the barn with a basket of carrots. The horses, happy to see their meal tickets, lowered their heads over the fence and swished their tails. Parks and Grant held the boys in their arms, guiding their hands.

Aunt Grace, still leery of the any livestock, much less the

horses, stood two feet back from the others. Not one to be shy, Bentley beckoned Aunt Grace closer. Her salt and pepper head barely topped the fence, but she inched closer to appease Bentley. Rebecca smiled as Henry went from Aunt Grace to Aunt Bell for more carrots as the horses hung their heads over the fence.

Just then, Henry turned towards them and squealed, "Daddy, look. Look at me feed the horsey."

Walker with the biggest grin on his face hollered back. "Good job, buddy."

As she'd predicted at the Fair on the Square, Walker had won over Aunt Grace. His love and dedication to Rebecca, especially since the birth of Henry, had proved to her aunt he was sincere.

As was the case when the uncles were in charge, a game of chase ensued. Grant and Parks chased Henry, who ran as fast as his chubby legs would take him. Bentley, ever the patient cousin, grabbed his hand to keep Henry steady as he ran.

Rebecca sighed at the sound of the boys' laughter. She had never imagined life could be this good. God had given her much more than she'd ever asked for or imagined. Walker kissed her forehead. "Happy?"

She turned in his arms. "I am. God has been so good to us, Walker."

He squeezed her tight and dropped a kiss on her forehead. "Thank you for saying 'I do.'"

"I'd do it all again if it meant I ended up with you."

His eyes crinkled as he gave her a kiss full of promise and commitment. Then he touched his forehead to hers. "You're right, He has. God is a good, good father."

She stepped back and placed his hand on her barely rounded stomach. "You will be too."

His eyes widened as she stared at him. "Wait. Are you saying what I think you're saying?"

She nodded.

A grin split his face as he picked her up and swung her around before shouting, "Look out, y'all, another Greystone is in the works."

She squeezed him tight. "I'm so glad our love found a home together."

* * * * *

Dear Reader,

Every mother wants to provide for her child. When Rebecca finds out that she's pregnant and unemployed, she's worried. Naturally so. Going so far as to move to a town with her ex's family to gain employment. Burdened by pain of past betrayals and a baby on the way, Rebecca is scared to try to love again. She feels abandoned and alone for most of her life. Yet, when Rebecca is in the hospital, she is able to reflect and see God has been by her side in each situation. She was not abandoned. God was there the whole time.

Meanwhile, Walker struggles with the burden of his father's mistakes, viewing himself through that flawed lens. The pressure to be perfect was unbearable, yet he tried. I love how Aunt Grace shares an eternal truth with him. That truth? God made us in His image. Once Walker embraced the truth, he found the courage to reach for a future he never thought he could have.

I love that once we get a true picture of who God is, we can walk in the confidence that we are loved and never alone!

I hope you enjoyed my debut novel. I would love to hear from you! Please visit me at alenaauguste.com.

Until then, may the Lord bless you and keep you.

Alena Auguste